Acknowledgements

As always there are a legion of people who contributed to this book. Dave Korte shared a story about his family's skunk farm, leading to an intriguing subplot. Julie Hovey continues to endure my distracted writing while she keeps our house and family together. Natalie Lund, the sentence structure and preposition rule enforcer, marked up a later draft and improved the readability of the book. Fran Brozo, and Clem MacIlravie catch plot issues and correct details specific to their background and experience. Anne Flagge and Deanna Wilson make a final post-editing sweep to catch the last typos, punctuation errors, misspellings, and truncated words. Without their dedicated assistance, the books would be much less than they are. Finally, thanks to J.D. Shipton, Jude Pittman, and the BWL editors for your contributions and continued support.

Skidded and Skunked
Pine County mystery #12

Dean L. Hovey
With D. L. Dixen

Print ISBNs
Amazon print 9780228634867
Ingram Spark 978-0-2286-3478-2
Audiobook 9780228634874
Barnes & Noble 9780228634881
BWL Print 9780228634898

This book is a work of fiction, a product of the authors' imaginations. Any resemblance to actual events, people, and locations is unintended and coincidental. The names of actual locations are used fictionally.

Dedication

To the boys in blue and brown who taught me real "cop stuff," both those still with us and those who watch over us from Above. My gratitude and love to all of you.
~ D.L. Dixen

"When someone is murdered, they always investigate the spouse, and that says all you need to know about marriage." - Mignon McLaughlin

"Farming is one of the few lines of work where living and employment conditions are mixed; in addition to agriculture workers, family members living on the farm are at risk for fatal and nonfatal injuries."
- US National Institute for Occupational Safety and Health (NIOSH)

Table of Contents

Prologue

June 24, 2023

Beroun is a small, unincorporated dot halfway between Pine City and Hinckley on a blue line marking old Highway 61. The hamlet consists of a few houses, a cement plant, and Maverick's Bar. It's a place mostly forgotten by the thousands of people driving north on I-35 to northern Minnesota resorts and summer cabins. To the locals, it is a hidden gem where they don't have to deal with city idiots.

On this particular Saturday night, Maverick's dozen bar stools were filled with people in jeans and t-shirts, their hands wrapped around Bootleggers, mugs of beer, or Jack and Cokes. Near the back of the bar, four men threw darts at an electronic board mounted on the knotty pine wall. Groups of laughing people surrounded the small tables. A waitress carrying a tray of deep-fried cheese curds and drinks threaded her way through a gauntlet of rowdy customers.

Corbin Baker and Carter Miller, young mechanics from a nearby car dealership, sat at a table with two empty chairs. They weren't laughing. Watching the door, Corbin frowned as a middle-aged couple walked in.

"If I could just talk to her, I'm sure we could sort things out."

"Dating a married woman is stupid, bruh. Either her husband found out and he's beaten her, or she's run away. She's history."

A few stools over, Craig and Donna Raster were drunk...again. Craig accused his wife of smiling at a guy throwing darts. Carter twisted to glare at them. "Hey, keep it down."

Craig turned to Carter and slurred, "You got a problem?"

"Just shut up, okay."

Raster started to stand, and his wife put her hand on his arm. "Leave it, Craig."

Turning away from the drunken couple, Corbin looked around the room. "Where's Casey tonight? He's usually here buying drinks for all of his prospective clients."

Carter took a breath, then finished his beer. "I'm outta here. This place is getting me down." He stood and walked out.

It took a minute for Carter's eyes to adjust to the dim parking lot lighting. With his brain fogged by beer, he wasn't sure where he'd parked. Standing on the wooden sidewalk, he scanned the array of pickups, motorcycles, 4-wheel ATVs, and cars. Spotting his rusty Dodge parked near the road, he threaded his way through the other vehicles. With his keys in his hand, he walked into the darkened space between his car and the Ford parked alongside it.

As he opened the driver's side door, a voice asked, "Do you have my money?" Unaware that anyone else was around, Carter spun toward the voice, losing his balance and catching himself on the vehicle's mirror. "I..."

"I told you my silence would be expensive. Today is payday, Miller. A couple thousand would keep me quiet until you can come up with the rest."

Sputtering and holding out his arm to distance himself from the man, he said, "I don't carry around that kind of money."

"I saw you at the ATM. Give me what's in your wallet as a downpayment."

Reaching for his wallet, he croaked, "I've got to pay..."

"You've got to pay me, is what you've got to do. Unless you'd rather have a discussion with the cops."

"No. No." Carter dropped his keys and fumbled with his wallet. Pulling out a handful of bills, he handed them to the man. "I'll get the rest later."

"When?"

"Maybe I can do installments."

The man laughed as he counted the money. "You've got until next Friday to come up with the other...four thousand, seven hundred and eighty bucks."

As quickly as he'd appeared, the man was gone. Carter put his empty wallet into his pocket and picked up his keys. Shaking, it took him nearly a minute to insert the key into the ignition. He sat with his hands on the steering wheel. *I'm screwed. There's no way in hell am I going to come up with that much money in a week.*

Chapter 1

May 9, 2025

Throughout her twenty-five-year marriage, Donna Raster had endured. It couldn't have been further from the idyllic, romantic partnership she'd been promised when she and Craig had first dated. Looking back, there had been hints of the hell she was about to live through. There was drinking and drugs. Then the verbal abuse shifted to physical assaults. Craig dragged her down the stairs by her hair. He'd thrown her through the glass patio door. Her injuries were always attributed to farm "accidents" if she was allowed medical attention. One nasty injury was blamed on a randy heifer who'd pinned her against the barn and broken her ribs. They told the ER doctor that one injury had been caused by a fall from the tractor while a broken jaw was blamed on a kick from a mean mama cow who didn't want Donna touching her calf. Craig told his drinking buddies his wife was lazy, stupid, and accident prone. Their dog received better treatment.

After he sobered up, Craig always apologized. Those apologies lasted until his next binge. And now, the binges were nearly every night. She'd thought about leaving, but where would she go? Craig had alienated them from her family and friends, leaving them only his drinking buddies as outside contacts, none of them sympathetic to Donna. Craig explained his behavior to anyone who would listen. "Sometimes Donna does the stupidest things. I'm a damned saint to put up with her shit. Anyone else would've gotten rid of her years ago."

Sitting at the kitchen table with her hand wrapped around a sweaty beer can, Donna stared out the window, watching Craig playing with his new toy. He'd explained it to her as if he was talking to a simple child. "It's a Bobcat skid steer. It has a front-end loader that can be swapped out with about a hundred different attachments."

"Why do you need a skid steer?" she'd asked.

Rolling his eyes, Craig snorted, "I just *told* you. It has a hundred uses. Hell, I'll be able to clear snow faster than ever. This spring, I'll get a post hole digger, and I'll replace all the fence posts along the driveway."

"We don't have money to buy beer. How can we afford it?"

That was the wrong question. The backhanded slap whipped her head around. She rubbed her sore neck at the memory.

Donna's ringtone sounded and she picked up the phone. "Get your butt out here. Let me show you what this baby will do to the manure pile."

Glancing out the window, she saw Craig motion for her to come outside. "I'm making supper," she lied.

"Now!"

Donna picked herself up out of the chair and walked to the entryway where she pulled on a threadbare Carhartt jacket and a pair of rubber barn boots. Trudging across the brown lawn, Donna walked into the barnyard and stopped next to the idling Bobcat. Crossing her arms, she asked, "What?"

"Come over here and look at these controls. This baby will turn on a dime." As Donna bent to look at the controls, Craig pushed the left lever to the side, causing the Bobcat to spin in one spot. Startled by the sudden movement, Donna jumped back, banging her head against the safety cage.

Stunned by the blow, Donna stumbled and fell to the ground in the muck. Pain replaced the numbness as she struggled to make sense of what had just happened. Blinking her eyes, she looked at the skid steer as it turned, rolled ahead, stopped, then backed up. She expected Craig to jump out and check on her. Instead, she heard the engine rev. Clawing desperately at the mud with her hands and heels, she tried to move herself out of the machine's path, only to slip and fall again. The tire ran over her hand, pinning her to the ground as she screamed for Craig to stop. As he continued backing up, her last thought was, *he really is going to kill me this time.*

Chapter 2

Pine County Sergeant CJ Jensen was parked on the Hinckley overpass with her radar gun trained on the I-35 traffic. It was pointless as the Minnesota fishing opener traffic was jammed up behind road construction. She watched as the backup spread farther to the south. Seeing the futility in running radar, she reached for the radio mic to announce her plan to resume patrol when the dispatcher called her number.

"Go ahead."

"We've got an ambulance call on Dahl Road, west of Hinckley. The caller reported a farm accident and requested an ambulance."

After acknowledging the call, CJ drove to the scene. Arriving well ahead of the Hinckley ambulance and firemen, she drove up the driveway toward a man waving his arms wildly in the barnyard. Approaching the man standing next to an open steel gate, she spotted a heap, dressed in a tan Carhartt coat, lying in the muddy stock pen behind him. "Come quick. Donna's hurt bad!"

Jogging toward the man, CJ assessed the scene. The Carhartt coat was stained with blood and muck. The rusty Bobcat skid steer was idling next to a body. The stench of diesel fumes, manure, and blood hit CJ's nose as she knelt behind the bloody heap. The victim faced away from her. She noticed long hair hinting it was a woman and recalled the man referred to her as 'Donna.' She wore rubber boots, a tan jacket and jeans. CJ extended her hand to check the victim's pulse. She hesitated when she realized half the woman's skull had been crushed. The woman had apparently tried to turn her head away from the approaching tires. Her open eyes were filled with terror and a silent scream hung on her open lips. CJ glanced at the husband and thought, *How could you have not heard her and stopped?*

Muddy tire tracks ran across the woman's arm, shoulder and the back of her head. It appeared the victim had possibly slipped and fallen in the mud. Her arm had been trapped under the tire as the machine backed over her, crushing her shoulder and skull. C.J. looked over the Bobcat's tire which was covered with blood and bits of tissue. She glared at the man and demanded, "What happened?"

"I dunno," the man replied, gesturing with his hands. "I was showing her how to run the skid steer. I told her to step back while I turned. Then, something happened. I think the controls got stuck in reverse. I couldn't see her and..." Unable to finish the sentence, the man shrugged.

Standing, CJ assessed the man's bloodshot eyes, grizzled graying beard, greasy hair, and dirty clothing. *Deadbeat* she thought to herself. She pointed to the still idling machine. "Shut it off."

"It's a diesel. You're supposed to let them run or..."

"Turn it off."

"To be honest, I'm not entirely sure how to do that. I don't suppose you, being a woman, would know how to do that."

Biting back what she really wanted to say after the sexist insult, CJ replied, "Try turning the key."

Confused, Raster looked side to side in the cab. "I don't remember where the key is."

Sighing, CJ pointed to the top right side of the cab. "It's up there."

Raster looked up, then reached for the ignition key. "I s'pose that might work," he said as the engine stopped.

The Hinckley fire truck turned into the driveway with the ambulance right behind it. The farmer looked at CJ and said, "I don't s'pose we'll be needing that ambulance."

Trying to retain her composure, CJ drew a breath. "I suppose not. Is anyone else home?"

"Nope. Just me and Donna here since Clarence died."

"Clarence?"

"My dog. He was a half St. Bernard, half black lab mix. The best dog I've ever had."

"Did the skid steer kill him too?"

The man scowled and shook his head. "Nope. He died of old age."

The firemen, dressed in their heavy bunker gear, jogged to the barnyard, followed by two ambulance attendants carrying first aid kits. The first fireman slipped in the mud and nearly fell. Standing next to CJ, he glanced at Donna's body, then shook his head before addressing the husband. "She really did it up good this time, Craig."

A second fireman went to Craig's side. "What happened?"

Craig froze. They waited for him to answer. "Well, I'm not entirely sure."

The closest fireman nodded. "I suppose you were backing up and she was looking away. The rear view in a Bobcat really sucks."

Craig quickly nodded. "Yeah, I was backing up. I didn't even know she was behind me until the Bobcat kinda thumped over her."

A third fireman approached the body and stood silently. He removed his helmet and bowed his head. The fourth fireman, barely out of his teens, stared at the woman's lifeless body, the blood draining from his face.

The first fireman slapped Craig on the back. "It's a damned shame. Doesn't look like this will be an open casket funeral." He looked at CJ. "Can I take Craig into the house? There's no point in standing out here in the cold and wind."

The second fireman nodded and turned to CJ. "Let me know when you're through. I'll go in and pour us a couple shots of Windsor to take the chill off."

The fireman with his head bowed, turned toward the husband and his two buddies. "Damn it! A woman is dead and you're laughing about a closed casket and throwing back a few shots. Shape up."

CJ stepped forward and gestured for the farmer to follow her to the gate. After radioing dispatch for an ETA on backup, she addressed the firemen, "Back away from the body and Bobcat."

The ambulance crew made a quick assessment of the victim's condition and confirmed that she was past any life-saving efforts. The lead attendant walked to CJ and sought direction. "Should we transport her directly to the funeral home, or do we need to take her to the hospital for an autopsy? It seems pretty evident that the cause of death was head trauma."

CJ turned to look at the scene. One of the firemen was standing next to the Bobcat and looked like he was preparing to climb in. Others were walking around the body and making tracks in the mud. "Hey! Listen up. This is a death scene. Everyone step away from the Bobcat and walk out of the pen. NOW!"

"It's obvious what happened," the first fireman protested. "There was an accident."

Putting on her best game face, CJ commanded, "We don't know what happened. Until I get a forensics team in here, we're treating this as a suspicious death. Get the hell out of the pen and secure the gate behind you."

The first firemen grumbled but moved away from the body. In a stage whisper, he said, "It must be her time of the month."

CJ pointed her finger at the culprit. "One more crack like that and I'll have a conversation with the fire chief."

The praying fireman grabbed the insolent fireman's arm. "Take it down a notch, Gary. Sergeant Jensen is doing her job."

Pointing at CJ, Gary replied, "She's acting like Craig killed Donna."

"Let her figure it out. Okay?"

Taking out her cell phone, CJ pulled Pam Ryan's number from her contacts. Pam answered on the first ring, "What's up?"

Focusing on the youngest fireman who had his helmet off and was leaning against a fence post, retching, CJ said, "I'm at a farm on Dahl Road, outside of Hinckley. A woman is dead in the pasture, and the husband appears under the influence and isn't troubled by the death. I'm not quite sure what I've got, but unless we get a medical examiner and BCA forensic team here ASAP, we'll never be able to prove it was anything but a tragic accident."

"Have you called anyone else yet?"

"Not yet. I've been trying to keep the husband separate from his firemen buddies while they feed him plausible stories and hurl sexist insults at me. Call the M.E. and the BCA."

"I'm on it. Do you want me to advise Floyd?"

In the distance, she saw the flashing lights of another Pine County Sheriff's Department SUV. She grimaced and said, "Perfect. Tell Floyd I could use some help with crowd control." Seeing the approaching flashing lights, she added, "and a babysitter for Riley."

"What's wrong?" Craig Raster asked as CJ ended the call.

"Nothing. Let's just wait here for a moment until my deputy arrives."

The newest Pine County Deputy Sheriff, Riley Sanders, stepped out of his SUV, adjusted his shiny new duty belt, then strutted up to CJ. "What do we have?"

"There's a dead woman in the pen. I'm going to interview the deceased woman's husband. While I'm doing that, keep the firemen and bystanders outside of the fence. Got it?"

"That's it? All you want me to do is keep people outside of the fence? I could start taking statements and collecting evidence."

"Riley, just keep everyone outside of the fence until the M.E. and BCA forensic team arrive."

"But..."

CJ stepped close to Riley and cut off his protest. "There's a dead woman inside of the fence and a half dozen people who want to go in and track up my crime scene. Keep everyone outside of the scene while I interview Mr. Raster. Got it?"

The stern tone of CJ's voice got Riley's attention. He nodded. "Yes, Sergeant."

Gesturing toward the house, CJ addressed the farmer, "I'll need your statement."

"I already said Donna was behind the Bobcat when the controls stuck."

"Let's go inside the house and fill in some of what happened before that. Okay?"

As CJ finished her sentence, she heard a faint buzzing sound off to her left. She quickly glanced up over her shoulder, didn't see anything, and continued on into the house.

Once inside, Raster took off his coat and kicked off his rubber barn boots in the mud room. CJ watched, then took out a pair of purple gloves to move the items aside. "I'll need your pants, too."

"What?"

"All your clothing needs to be collected for evidence. Take off your pants."

Raster's eyes narrowed. "You make it sound like I killed Donna."

"I'm not saying anything except that we need your clothing for forensic analysis."

Unbuckling his Smith & Wesson belt buckle, Raster glared at CJ. "This is harassment."

"No, this is proper police procedure."

Raster's lips curled into a sneer. "I ain't wearing underwear. Are you just going to stare?"

Making a spinning gesture with her hand, CJ said, "Face away from me if you're shy, but you're not leaving my presence until I have your pants."

"You're kind of pushy," Raster said as he unzipped, then lowered his jeans, exposing a pair of dingy, threadbare briefs with a urine stain. "Do you want my underwear too?"

"No, you need them more than I do." Nodding toward a pair of bib overalls, CJ suggested he put them on. Folding the jeans, she set them on top of the jacket. "How much have you had to drink today?"

"Why do you care? It's not like I've been driving on the road," he slurred. Thus, confirming what CJ already knew. He was, in fact, drunk. She would need to PBT him to get a precise reading.

Chapter 3

Pam leaned her elbows against the fence post supporting the gate, inhaling the scent of cattle, cow pies, mud, and diesel exhaust. The medical examiner had just removed the body while she was mentally reviewing what she and CJ had just witnessed. Several curious steers watched from beyond the fence as they chewed their cud.

The Bobcat sat in a sea of mud, awaiting the Bureau of Criminal Apprehension forensic team. Aside from that, the muddy pen looked like any other barnyard in the Midwest.

"What are you thinking?" CJ asked, pulling Pam back from her daydream.

"Did you know that farming is one of the most dangerous occupations?"

Leaning alongside Pam on the metal gate, CJ replied, "It can be. When you look at the OSHA analysis of workplace deaths, farming is right up there next to construction and transportation workers. Considering how few farmers there are..."

"We respond to a few farm accidents a year." Pam stared at the spot where Donna Raster's body had rested, trying to visualize the events leading to her death. "Do you think this was a tragic accident?"

"I'm not so sure. Craig is drunk. He blew a .19 on the breathalyzer—more than twice the legal limit. I don't know if the alcohol dampened his emotions or if there is something else, but he doesn't seem torn up enough about Donna's death. He didn't even have a plausible explanation about what happened until one of the stupid firemen suggested the Bobcat had a blind spot and Donna was out of his sight." CJ shook her head.

"Okay, let's review what we know," Pam suggested.

"Craig was drunk. He didn't have an explanation of how the events unfolded until one was suggested to him. He didn't seem sad. Do you know anything more?"

"The Bobcat was moved after it ran over Donna."

"What?" CJ questioned.

Pam nodded toward the Bobcat. "I looked at the tires. It appears the Bobcat tires backed over the victim, then pulled ahead again in a slightly different line, then backed up to where it's parked." She drew a breath and blew it out again, as if dealing with a wave of nausea. "There's blood and brain tissue in the tire tracks both in front of and behind where the victim died and where the Bobcat is now parked."

"You photographed that, right?"

"I did but it's more difficult to discern the tire pattern and tissue from photos than it is to see it."

"Craig said he'd never operated a skid steer before today. I suppose he might've panicked after he hit Donna and pushed the wrong lever."

"Is that what he told you?" Pam asked.

"No. Between the alcohol and shock, he can't remember exactly what happened. He initially said the controls stuck."

"Even in that state, you'd think he might remember feeling the bump when he ran over his wife repeatedly."

"Yeah. You'd think something like that would stick in your mind. Unless he's lying."

Pam turned to look at the barn and house. "I don't suppose there's a camera overlooking the scene."

"I think a security camera might've been a little more technology than Craig Raster could handle," CJ snorted.

"He's not the sharpest knife in the drawer?" Pam asked.

"Using the silverware analogy, I'd say there are spoons sharper than Craig."

"I ran his '45. He's had three DUIs and been through both in and outpatient alcohol treatment."

CJ nodded toward the house. "The recycling bin is full of beer cans. They've either been accumulating for a long time, or the Rasters consume a LOT of beer."

"It sounds like maybe Craig has been missing some court-mandated AA meetings." Pam looked to the left and right. "The farm north of here is vacant with a For Sale sign out front. I'll ask Raster's southern neighbors if they saw or heard anything."

CJ looked down the driveway. "There's nothing but cattails across the road. I don't suppose some hunter has a camera watching a game trail over there."

"Is that a hint that I should slog through the swamp in search of a camera?"

CJ smiled. "I'm the senior officer. Don't bother checking the swamp. I'll have Riley take a walk back there."

"That'd be a cruel thing to do to the rookie."

Raising her eyebrows, CJ replied. "I could let you do it if you wanted."

"No, no. That's a perfect job for 'Mr. Eager'. Make sure he covers himself with mosquito and tick repellent before he walks in. I wouldn't want him to get Lyme disease or Zika virus."

* * *

Pam noticed a pickup in the neighbor's yard, so she pulled in and parked. The back door opened as she announced her location to the dispatcher. The smiling gray-haired woman waved from the steps, then grabbed the railing to steady herself as she stepped down. Pam had taken one step when motion behind the woman's feet caught her eye. Expecting a dog or cat, Pam was shocked when she recognized the black coat and white stripes of a skunk.

From twenty feet away, Pam called out, "Ma'am, there's a skunk behind you."

The woman put her hand to her ear, apparently unable to discern Pam's warning.

Yelling louder, Pam repeated, "There's a skunk behind you!"

The woman looked down and then glanced over her shoulder. Apparently undisturbed by the skunk's presence, she continued walking toward Pam.

Taking a step backward, Pam stumbled and fell against her squad. She quickly pushed herself up and reached for the door.

"It's okay," the woman called, still smiling. "It's just Stinky."

Pausing with her hand on the door handle, Pam asked, "Stinky?"

"She's a harmless pet. Don't worry, Stinky's descented."

Not entirely at ease, Pam stood next to the squad, keeping her hand on the door handle. "Does Stinky bite?"

"Heavens no. Stinky is friendly."

The woman stopped at the front fender of Pam's squad, but Stinky continued on until she was sniffing Pam's shoes. Still uneasy about the prospect of being sniffed by a skunk, Pam asked, "Can you call Stinky? I'm not really a skunk person."

The woman approached Pam, then held out half a dozen brown pellets. "Feed her some cat chow. Stinky will be your friend for life."

"I think the department has guidelines about feeding wildlife."

"Stinky isn't wild at all. She's more docile than my cat." The woman reached out and placed the pellets in Pam's palm. "Just hold them out. I wouldn't recommend holding them in your fingers because she's a little near-sighted and might nip your fingertips."

Shuddering, Pam stared at the pellets, then at Stinky, who had apparently discerned the transfer of food to Pam. Stinky jumped up on her hind feet and appeared to be begging for the food while making a raspy snuffling sound. "I..."

"There's nothing to be afraid of, dear. Stinky is vaccinated and completely harmless."

Grimacing, Pam extended her palm to the skunk, who pulled it down with her front paws. The skunk's rough tongue tickled Pam's palm as she ate the pellets. "How long have you had Stinky?"

"This is actually Stinky the fourth. Skunks have a shorter lifespan than dogs or cats." The woman smiled and introduced herself. "I'm Marvel Erickson."

"Pam Ryan. I'm an investigator with the Pine County Sheriff's Department."

"I saw all the commotion over at the Raster place. I assume something bad happened to Donna."

"Why would you assume that?"

"I sometimes hear them shouting at each other. I can't make out the words, but I can tell that their arguments are heated."

"Do you know the Rasters well?"

"Not at all. They didn't do much with the neighbors. Mostly we'd wave when passing each other on the road."

"Did you notice anything happening today?"

Marvel glanced toward her neighbor's house, a half mile away. "Do you mean before the police cars and ambulance arrived?"

"Yes. I'd like to know what happened earlier today."

A frown creased Marvel's brow. "Do you have time for a cup of coffee?"

Knowing the coffee invitation was the Pine County version of, *I'd like to tell you something,* Pam nodded. "Sure."

Stinky followed them to the house, sometimes circling around Pam's feet making a snuffling sound. At the steps, Stinky left them and bounded into the long grass behind the house.

Pam was engulfed by the aroma from a Dutch oven cooking on the stove as she stepped inside. "Mmm. Something smells amazing."

"I've got a pot of stew cooking. It's a modified Julia Child recipe. She uses a lot of thyme, onions, and red wine."

Marvel pulled a chair back from the kitchen table and gestured for Pam to take a seat. Gathering mugs from the cupboard, then the coffee carafe from the machine, Marvel set them on the table. She slumped into the chair as if her legs had stopped working. Pam waited for her to speak. "You know that Craig and Donna *got into it* once in a while?"

"They had physical altercations?"

Marvel nodded as she poured coffee into the mugs. "Is 'physical altercation' a euphemism for 'he beat the shit out of her?'"

Accepting the coffee mug, Pam smiled. "Is that what happened?"

"Personally, I think Donna gave back as much as she got. She wasn't a shrinking violet."

"Did you ever try to intervene?"

Marvel sipped her coffee before replying. "Craig and Donna were not interested in being neighborly."

"Did they tell you that?"

"The letter carrier delivered some of their mail to me shortly after they moved here. I brought it over with a plate of homemade cookies. Donna thanked me, but she made it clear they weren't going to invite me over for Thanksgiving."

"How did you determine that Donna was being abused?"

"When you can hear the yelling from this far away, it's pretty clear they've escalated past throwing insults." Marvel paused, then added, "I saw Craig knock her down once. Then he got in his pickup and drove away."

"Did you call 911?"

Marvel shrugged. "Craig left. There wasn't any point. Besides, when I called about someone breaking into my barn, it took nearly an hour for a deputy to respond. If I were being attacked, I'd have been dead, and my killer would've been halfway to Canada."

"Yeah, our response times are a bit long if we've got a call on the other end of the county." Pam paused, then asked, "Did you hear them fighting today?"

"No, not today. I didn't hear anything until the sirens raced by me. Oh, and your buzzing flying machine."

Noticing a skunk skin draped over the back of a chair in the living room adjacent to the kitchen, Pam asked, "Is that Stinky the third?"

"That one didn't have a name."

"You've had unnamed pet skunks?"

A smile creased Marvel's face, accentuating the natural crow's feet at the corners of her eyes. "If you've got a minute, I'd like to show you my barn."

"What's in your barn? Wait. Buzzing flying machine?" Something clicked in Pam's mind then was gone.

"The skunk operation," Marvel replied. With considerable effort, Marvel pushed herself up from the chair using the table and the chair back.

Pam followed her host down a well-worn path from the house to the barn. At some point, Stinky appeared from the long weeds and joined them. After unlocking a padlock, Marvel led Pam into an old dairy barn filled with an obvious skunk odor. She flipped the light switch and animals started moving inside cages, the sound of dozens of snuffling skunks filled the space.

"Is there much demand for pet skunks?" Pam asked, looking at the dozens of cages with a variety of skunks from kits to adults with graying muzzles. Some had nearly black coats with only a narrow white stripe, others were nearly half white.

"What are the black skunks?"

"They're a genetic anomaly. It's very popular and I'm trying to push the limits of white and pure black."

"They're all pets?"

"I get orders for a few. I only sell the most docile ones as pets. Most of these are fur animals."

"There's a market for skunk fur?"

"Wearing fur is still big in Eastern Europe. And there's a novelty market in the US for skunk-skin hats. You know, like Davy Crockett, only with skunks instead of raccoons."

Sniffing the air, Pam wrinkled her nose. "How do you deal with the scent?"

"I remove the scent glands from the kits. Even with the sprayer removed, they have a bit of residual musky scent."

"Thanks for the tour. I should be on my way."

Following Pam out and locking the barn, Marvel stopped at Pam's squad. "If you're not in a hurry, I've got stew cooking."

"Thanks, but I'll eat with my family."

"I made a huge batch. Can I put some into a Tupperware for you?"

"I really can't accept a gift."

"Most people wouldn't call skunk stew a gift. Come on into the house, I'll put some in a container."

Nearly sickened by the thought of skunk stew, Pam hesitated. "Skunk stew?"

"The meat is white and mild. Most people can't tell it's not pork."

"Thanks, but I really can't accept any gifts."

"I won't tell anyone you got a quart of stew from me," Marvel said, reveling in Pam's discomfort. "Take some home to your family. You don't have to tell them it's made with skunk until after they've eaten it."

"I don't think that's a good idea. Besides, the department has a strict policy against accepting gifts. Thank you. But no."

A Pine County SUV pulled into the driveway as the two women stood by Pam's SUV. Marvel's eyes lit up. "Wow, I haven't had this much company since the Ukrainian fur buyers were here."

Deputy Riley Sanders parked alongside Pam's vehicle, then joined them. "Hi, Pam. CJ said you had something I needed to do here."

Momentarily drawing a blank after the skunk stew discussion, Pam had to think back to her conversation with CJ. "Yes. We need you to check the acreage on the other side of the road for game cameras."

Glancing over his shoulder at the cattail-filled ditch across the road, Riley sighed. "There aren't any game cameras in those cattails." Turning back, he was quickly distracted by movement in the long grass. His eyes went wide, and he reached for his pistol. "Skunk!"

"Stand down, rookie!" Pam commanded. "That's a pet skunk." She reached down to pet Stinky.

With his hand still on the butt of his pistol, Riley watched. "I've never heard of a pet skunk."

"Mrs. Erickson breeds them."

Marvel, obviously having some pain in her joints, used the handrail to ease back down the steps. She took a handful of cat chow pellets from her pocket and held them out to Riley. "Put some in your palm and Stinky will be your friend for life."

Reluctantly, Riley took the pellets and bent down, extending his hand to the skunk.

Stinky waddled over and quickly devoured the treat.

Pam sniffed the air and smiled at the homeowner as a plan formed. "Mrs. Erickson, do you have enough stew to feed Deputy Sanders?"

Marvel smiled and played along. "I've got a big pot of stew. Would you like to join me for supper, Deputy?"

Riley sensed he was about to be the victim of another rookie prank but couldn't discern what it might be. Riley smiled and introduced himself. "It's almost the end of my shift and I was going to stop for a burger. I'd love a bowl of homemade stew. It smells wonderful."

Marvel nodded toward the steps and said, "Come on in. I'll ladle up a couple bowls of stew for us. I've got homemade bread to go with it."

Riley stopped at Pam's shoulder and asked, "You're not having any of the stew?"

"I've got a husband and kid at home," she said as they passed. "I can't hang around socializing like you single guys."

"Is it okay if I eat before checking for cameras?"

"The cameras will be there whenever you get to them. Just remember to ask to use Mrs. Erickson's bathroom before you check the cameras. You wouldn't want to be on the roll of some hunter's footage," Pam snorted as she hurried to her cruiser.

Careful not to run over Stinky IV, Pam backed out of the driveway as quickly as she could. *OMG. Just wait until CJ and Floyd hear about Riley eating skunk stew.* Her second thought was, *Travis would kill me if I fed him skunk stew, no matter how good it smelled.*

Chapter 4

Craig Raster's story nagged at CJ as she drove towards Pine City. His lack of grief weighed heavily on her mind. He might've been in shock, but he didn't seem upset enough about his wife's death. Something was off about the whole scenario.

After retrieving Bailey from doggie daycare, CJ heated a frozen pot pie in the microwave and fed the dog. Bailey sniffed the dog food and sat down. Her sad eyes fixed on CJ, who was leaning against the kitchen counter waiting for the microwave to beep.

"What? You're too good for dry dog food? I'm not buying canned dog food, Basset."

The microwave beeped and CJ used hot pads to move the pot pie to a plate. The dog continued to stare at her as she transferred the plate to her tiny kitchenette. With the pot pie still too hot to eat, CJ took a tumbler from the cupboard and drew herself a glass of water. When she turned, Bailey had her nose on the table, sniffing the pot pie, preparing to jump onto her chair.

"Don't even think about it," CJ said as she rushed to the table to pull the chair away from the dog. The basset slumped to the floor and rested her head on her massive paws. CJ retrieved the remote from the couch and turned the TV news on. Halfway through the CBS network broadcast about unrest in the Middle East, the station cut away to breaking local news. A header read *Pine County aerial video of farm accident*. "We've just received this drone footage of a farm accident in rural Pine County. We've dispatched a reporter to get the full story. As of now, all we have is this video taken by a local viewer earlier today who saw the Pine County Sheriff's Department and the Hinckley Fire Department responding to a reported farm accident. Our source said one person is dead. We assume the deceased person is under the blue tarp behind the barn. We're waiting for a return call from the sheriff's department spokesperson."

"What drone?" CJ asked Bailey, tipping her head as she pictured the farm and the barnyard. After a second, her eyes popped open. "That was the buzzing sound I heard!"

Hearing the excitement in her owner's voice, Bailey's tail started thumping the floor. The words were barely out of CJ's mouth before her cell phone buzzed. The caller ID read PCSD.

"Where are you?" the sheriff's bass voice asked.

"I'm sitting at my kitchen table with a hot dinner in front of me."

"Throw it into the refrigerator and put on a fresh uniform. We're being interviewed about the farm death. Meet me on the courthouse steps in fifteen minutes."

"You don't need me."

"Listen, Charlene, you're the face the viewers expect to see next to me. You represent the next generation of Pine County Sheriff's Department leadership."

CJ looked at Bailey, setting off another round of tail thumping. "Pam was there, too."

"I'm sure she's at home eating supper with her husband and son. You only live five minutes from the courthouse."

"I'm ten minutes away. Twenty after I shower, change into a uniform, and jam my hair under a cap."

"Skip the shower. The cameras can't smell you."

"I smell like a barnyard," CJ lied, having showered after picking up Bailey.

"Bullshit! You wouldn't prepare supper still stinking of manure. You've wasted two of your twenty minutes arguing with me. Get your butt over here. Now!"

"But I don't know anything," she protested. Only after the words were out did she realize the sheriff had ended the call. Biting back an expletive, CJ dumped the pot pie on top of the dog food. "It's your lucky day, dog," she said to Bailey as she walked into the bedroom to change.

* * *

The news media were gathering on the east side of the Pine County courthouse when CJ parked near the lower-level sheriff's department entrance. Bracing herself for the unpleasant task of facing the reporters, CJ rode the elevator to the upper level and walked out of the main courthouse doors. The sheriff was speaking with a young blonde reporter holding a digital voice recorder. John Sepanen excused himself and met her at the door.

"Cutting it a little close," he said, while smiling at the crowd.

"Unless you wanted me to show up in jeans and a sweatshirt, I got here as quickly as I could."

"Are we calling this an accident, or something else?"

"At this point, the cause of death is under investigation."

"What's your gut say?"

CJ paused. "With all due respect, sir, I don't want my gut feelings shared with the news media."

The comment caught the sheriff by surprise. "I never..."

"You always say what's on your mind. If my gut feeling is the last input you've had, it may be what you share with this fine group of news people." She forced a smile as they spoke.

Forcing himself to smile as if he and CJ were having a polite conversation, the sheriff replied, "I don't share speculation with the media."

"No? You often say an arrest is imminent when we don't have a clue what in hell is going on," CJ countered, while continuing to flash a fake smile.

"That's what they expect. And to be honest, my deputies rarely let me down."

"Fine. Our investigation is awaiting autopsy results and testing from the BCA," CJ spat through gritted teeth.

Her reaction was one of surprise when the sheriff responded, "You don't think it was an accident?"

"Most people don't *accidentally* run over their victim three times, sir."

The smile disappeared from the sheriff's face. "He ran her over three times? Jesus, Mary, and Joseph."

Gesturing toward the array of microphones, CJ said, "I'd avoid blasphemy when speaking to the media. It might tarnish your image with the voters." Her phony smile returned.

"Not only the voters. I'd be saying Hail Mary's for a month after Father Mike got through with me."

"You ought to convert to Lutheranism. We just pray for forgiveness."

Moving toward the microphones the sheriff asked, "And when was the last time you attended a Lutheran service?"

"Point taken, sir."

Composing himself, the sheriff took a breath and smiled as he looked at the gathered reporters and videographers. "As you may have heard, a Pine County resident lost their life during a farm incident today. The victim's identity is confidential pending notification of family members. I can say that the incident involved a piece of farm equipment." Turning to CJ, he continued, "Sergeant Jensen was the incident commander and will be making a comment."

After giving the sheriff a look that would melt steel, CJ stepped up to the microphones. "There's quite a bit we don't know. A person was killed by a piece of farm equipment this afternoon. An autopsy will be performed by the Duluth Medical Examiner's Office and the Minnesota Bureau of Criminal Apprehension is examining the scene and equipment involved."

"Was it an accident?" A woman's voice yelled from the crowd.

"I can't comment on an ongoing investigation."

"Did it look like an accident?" the woman said, restating her question.

"It was a tragic death. I can't comment on it at this time."

A male voice called out from the crowd, "We heard that the victim's husband was drunk when he ran over her. Can you confirm that?"

"I can't comment on that."

The man reiterated, "A fireman said you ran a breathalyzer on him at the scene."

"We routinely assess all people involved in a fatality."

"Even if they're sober?" a female reporter asked. That question generated a titter of laughter.

"Everyone involved in a fatality is assessed for impairment per department policy."

Apparently feeling that CJ was stealing his spotlight, the sheriff stepped forward. "It is our department's policy to evaluate everyone involved in a fatal incident, whether it happens on the highway or on a farm. Sergeant Jensen was following our department protocol. We won't have the results of that assessment for several days." The sheriff raised his hands. "I'm afraid that's all the information we can share. Thanks for your patience."

The sheriff guided CJ into the courthouse and closed the doors, cutting off the questions and ending their coverage. "A fireman told a reporter that the Bobcat's operator was drunk?"

"I can't control what a volunteer fireman says," CJ replied. "That comment doesn't surprise me. The fire department first responders seemed to know the victim and her husband. They were kidding him about finally being rid of her."

"The hell you say?"

"Yup. Rigor mortis hadn't set in, and they were joking about him killing her."

Running his hand over his face, the sheriff grimaced. "This is going to be a disaster."

"Maybe you should've delayed the news coverage until we actually knew something."

Sepanen stiffened. "If anyone but you said that to me, I'd be chewing their ass."

"Floyd told me that someone has to be willing to tell you when you've done something stupid or have gone too far. He's not here, so I guess it's up to me."

Gesturing toward the elevator, the sheriff led CJ away from the front of the building. "As much as it pains me to agree with that comment, Floyd is usually right." Stepping into the elevator the sheriff turned to CJ as the doors closed. "It's never wrong for you to tell the emperor he's not wearing any clothes. If you repeat that statement, I'll deny it. I grant you permission to pull me aside to tell me that I'm being an ass. My only request is that you do it behind closed doors."

CJ smiled as the elevator doors opened. "It'll be my pleasure, sir."

Seeing a jailer standing nearby, the sheriff cut off his response.

* * *

After tossing and turning that night, CJ slipped on a pair of jeans and sweatshirt to go for a walk. Bailey opened one eye to watch the process but made no move to join her owner. At the front door, CJ clipped a holster onto her jeans and pulled the hem of the sweatshirt over the pistol. After taking the leash down from the hook next to the door, she looked around for the dog.

"Bailey, get your butt out here."

The sound of groaning came from the bedroom, followed by the basset expelling a loud fart. A moment later, the jingling of Bailey's dog tags announced her procession down the hallway. She paused, assessing her owner's seriousness about a midnight stroll.

"Come on. We're walking." CJ knelt down and opened the clip on the leash. With excessive effort, Bailey waddled across the room and stopped just close enough for CJ to attach the leash to her harness.

Once outside, CJ led the basset down the sidewalk toward the nearby residential neighborhood. It was their usual route, offering an assortment of signposts and fire hydrants for Bailey to sniff while CJ verbalized her thoughts. After confirming there was no one nearby to hear her, CJ spoke while the dog thoroughly examined the base of a speed limit sign.

"The whole scene was off," CJ explained to the dog, who ignored her. "According to everything I saw, Raster ran over his wife with his Bobcat. He didn't seem at all traumatized by her death. When the firemen arrived, they joked with him about finally being rid of his wife. It was as if he'd talked about killing her over a beer. Very few of them seemed surprised or even upset."

Satisfied that she'd discerned all of the odors at the signpost, Bailey started down the sidewalk toward a mailbox.

"Not that the firemen were a great source of information. I've rarely been the subject of so many inappropriate comments since junior high school. One of them even told the others I was cranky because I had my period."

When CJ stopped speaking, Bailey turned her head as if she'd heard something unbelievable.

"I know, no one has used that line on me in twenty years." Bailey started walking and CJ added, "The guy was a sexist jerk. I was the only law enforcement person on the scene, so I was obviously in charge. Yet, he was busting my chops because I was asserting authority. What are they? A good old boys' club who don't recognize women in leadership roles?"

A cottontail rabbit ran out from behind a bush and Bailey lunged after it, nearly dislocating CJ's shoulder.

Regaining her balance, CJ grabbed the leash with both hands and planted her feet. "No! Stop, Basset!"

Undeterred, Bailey strained at the leash, trying to pursue the rabbit. Even after the animal disappeared through the lattice under a nearby porch, she continued to strain at the leash.

CJ pulled the hound back until they were in the same concrete square. "Here's the deal. You couldn't catch the bunny even if you were off the leash. If you did catch the bunny, you wouldn't know what to do with it."

Bailey finally relented and sat down with a grunt.

"It's the same thing with those firemen. They were talking big about Craig 'getting rid of his wife.' I doubt any of them has the guts to confront their wives over their *perceived* issues, much less acting out their juvenile threats."

Chapter 5

The next morning, Pam, who was sitting at her desk in the bullpen, turned when she heard CJ pop a pod into the Keurig coffee maker. "I've got some makeup that would hide those bags under your eyes," Pam said, smiling.

Leaning against the counter, CJ looked too tired to reply. "It was a short night."

"Did the dog keep you awake?"

CJ gestured with her fingers. "Don't you have a form to fill out or something, Blondie?"

"There's no rush."

After removing the coffee cup, CJ sat down at the nearest desk. "I'm too tired to joke around."

The dispatcher stuck her head around the corner, "CJ, you've got a call on the non-emergency line."

Without lifting the phone receiver, CJ put the call on the speaker. "This is Sergeant Jensen."

A male voice asked, "Are you CJ?"

"I'm *Sergeant* Jensen."

"Um, you were at Rasters' farm yesterday, right?"

"I was. What can I do for you?"

"I'm Ernie Sternquist, one of the firemen who responded. I was wondering if we could meet for a cup of coffee?"

"Do you have some information about the events at the farm?"

"Well, not really information. I was kind of hoping we could have a cup and talk."

Frowning, CJ looked at Pam who had stopped typing and was listening. "Is this related to Donna Raster's death or something else?"

Ernie cleared his throat. "Can we just meet?"

"I'd like to know why, Ernie."

"I can't really say over the phone. Maybe I could buy you a cup of coffee at the Whistlestop Café."

Checking the clock, CJ replied, "I can be there in twenty minutes or so."

"That'd be great. I'll see you then."

Ending the call, CJ shook her head. "That was odd."

A grin spread across Pam's face. "I know who Ernie is. He's the middle-aged fireman with the aw-shucks kind of mannerism. He told me he was a widower."

CJ closed her eyes and grimaced. "Did you tell him I was a widow?"

"It might've come up."

"What the hell, Pam?"

"Don't put this on me. I was just making conversation. He said you were kind of cute."

Sighing, CJ pushed herself out of the chair. "You owe me a week of dog sitting for this."

Pam shoved her chair into her desk and yelled after CJ, "How about you watch your own damn dog for a change?"

CJ snorted and waved over her shoulder. "Come on. Don't you want to be a great investigator? Even Columbo had a basset!"

Pam blew out a breath and threw up a hand gesture she had learned in *Skills* with the other trainees. CJ's footsteps, intermixed with her laughter, echoed through the hallway as she retreated to her squad.

Pam had just refocused on her report when a skunk smell assaulted her nose. Turning toward the door, she saw Riley standing in the hallway looking sheepish. "Is that stink coming from you?"

"I showered," he replied defensively.

"Try bathing in a couple gallons of tomato juice, then come back tomorrow."

Floyd walked out of his office holding his nose. "What in hell happened to you?"

"You told me to check for game cameras across the road from the Rasters' farm yesterday. I saw a skunk and thought it was the pet skunk from Mrs. Erickson's place. You know, the one who eats cat food out of your hand?"

Pointing toward the exit, Floyd said, "Buy a pint of hydrogen peroxide, a scrub brush, and a bottle of dishwashing detergent. Mix a tablespoon of detergent and all the peroxide in a gallon of water and scrub yourself until you don't stink anymore."

"I'll do that at the end of my shift," Riley said.

"Do it now!" Floyd replied, continuing to point toward the exit. "Afterwards, have someone sniff your squad to see if it needs to be deodorized too."

"I can do that myself," Riley replied as he retreated toward the door.

"Your sniffer is shot. Have someone else see if the seats need to be deodorized."

Unable to stifle her laughter, Pam chuckled. "We may have to get the hallway fumigated."

* * *

Arriving at the Whistlestop Café twenty minutes later, CJ scanned the sidewalk and parked cars for the middle-aged fireman she'd seen at the farm. Her plan to intercept him before being trapped into having a cup of coffee with him failed, so she stepped inside the eatery. There was no problem identifying the fireman because he waved excitedly from a table in the middle of the room.

In a gentlemanly gesture, Ernie stood and pulled out a chair for CJ. "Thanks for coming. I'm Ernie Sternquist."

"I can only stay a minute or two."

"I suppose you're a busy person, Sergeant. I just wanted a moment of your time."

The waitress arrived with a steaming cup of coffee. She winked at Ernie as she set it in front of CJ.

"You said you had something important to say that couldn't be discussed over the phone."

Ernie nervously picked at the scab on his earlobe. "In all honesty, that was a white lie. I wanted to buy you a cup of coffee and apologize for some of the stupid things my crew said at Rasters' farm. You handled things well. You seem like a confident person, and I haven't met many women like you."

"Thanks for the apology."

Ernie fidgeted with his cup. "I'm a widower..."

CJ held up one finger. "Ernie, thank you for the coffee. I agreed to meet you because you indicated you had information on the Raster case. I don't mean to sound harsh, however, I need to get back to patrol. What was it you couldn't share with me over the phone?"

Grimacing, Ernie drew a breath. "I just want to have a cup of coffee with an intelligent woman..." He trailed off when CJ held his gaze.

"Beyond their sexist remarks, some of the firemen made some rather incriminating statements at Rasters' farm. Has Craig really been telling people he was going to kill his wife?"

"This wasn't exactly the kind of conversation I was hoping to have," Ernie replied as he continued to pick at the scab.

"You wanted to speak with someone who acted professionally."

After taking a sip of coffee to compose his thoughts, Ernie said, "Craig mouths off quite a bit, like a lot of the guys. None of them are seriously considering acting out the stupid macho things they talk about. It's usually just the alcohol talking."

"Boys being boys?"

"Yeah," Ernie replied. "It sometimes gets out of hand."

"But Craig has said he'd like to be rid of Donna, right?"

Ernie blew out a breath and clenched his eyes. "I never said this, okay? He's mouthed off about a lot of things including throwing Donna out."

Taking out a pen and notepad, CJ asked, "Who were the firemen at Raster's place?"

Ernie squirmed in his chair. "They won't be happy about me ratting on them."

"It's a matter of public record. Either you tell me, or I'll pull the fire department log." CJ waited a moment, making sure Ernie was going to respond, then suggested, "Start with the loudmouth who told Craig how the 'accident' occurred."

"Let's see. That would've been Gary Proctor. He's got a mouth on him, and no one wonders what's on his mind."

"Okay, who was the quiet kid who tossed his cookies?"

Ernie chuckled at the thought. "That's Kyle Butcher. He's our newest volunteer. He's still learning the ropes."

"And the other middle-aged guy?"

"Oliver Benton."

"Tell me about Oliver."

Ernie shrugged. "There's not much to say. Ollie's an average guy."

"Does he drink with Craig and Gary?"

"Yeah, he's part of the bar crew. They're drinking together most Friday nights."

"What's their favorite watering hole?"

"There's a bar down the block from the fire hall. It's gone by a couple of different names over the years. It's called Smokie's now."

After closing her notebook and glancing at her watch, CJ took a sip of coffee. "Thanks for the coffee. I need to be in Duluth in an hour."

Ernie stood and threw a twenty-dollar bill on the table. "Let me walk you out."

"You don't need to do that."

"Please."

Feeling like every eye was on them, CJ walked ahead of Ernie to the door. "Thank you, Ernie." CJ was about to turn away when a wild thought occurred to her. "Does your department ever recruit new firefighters?"

"We always need a few more people. Are you thinking about becoming a volunteer fireman?"

"I live too far away. However, we've got a rookie deputy who's trying to become more engaged in the community. Who should I have him call?"

Ernie pulled a pen from his breast pocket. "If you've got a business card, I'll write my number down. He can call me." After scrawling the number on CJ's card, Ernie handed it to her. "If you ever want to have another cup of coffee, you could call that number yourself."

"I'll keep that in mind."

Climbing into her squad, CJ felt as if she'd dodged a bullet. Driving out of Hinckley, CJ's cell phone rang. Without checking the caller ID she answered, "Sergeant Jensen."

"Tony's ahead of schedule," Eddie, the medical examiner's assistant said. "How soon can you be at the morgue?"

"I'm in Hinckley, it'll take me an hour if I speed."

"I'll stall as best I can."

Ending that call, CJ punched in Floyd's number. "I think Riley is going to do an undercover assignment."

Floyd snorted. "Do you think that's wise?"

"I've got the phone number for the Hinckley fire chief. If Riley volunteers with them, he could find out what the firemen know about Craig Raster's intent in his wife's death."

"I'm not sure he's ready to handle anything that delicate," Floyd replied.

"All he's got to do is show up at the meetings and go out on fire calls when he's off duty with us. How hard can that be?"

"Think about what you just said. We're talking about Riley. He could mess up an order for a cup of black coffee. You might want to stay clear of the bullpen until we get it fumigated. Riley wasn't smart enough to avoid a skunk while he was looking for game cameras."

Sighing, CJ replied, "Think about putting Riley undercover with the fire department. I'm on my way to Duluth for Donna Raster's autopsy."

Chapter 6

CJ parked in a spot reserved for police vehicles outside of the Duluth hospital and walked to the M.E.'s office. The reception desk was unattended, so she went directly to the morgue. Inside she found Tony Oresek, the M.E., standing next to a table where Donna Raster's body was laid out.

Eddie Paulson looked up from a microscope on a countertop. "The disposable coveralls and masks are in the usual spot," he said.

Apparently annoyed, the M.E. looked up from his examination of the woman's body. "You don't need to wear your bulletproof vest here. Neither Eddie, nor I, will shoot you."

Releasing the Velcro straps, CJ slipped the vest over her head and chose a set of white coveralls from a cubbyhole. "What have I missed?"

"We took x-rays and I've removed a lot of barnyard dirt and manure from the surface of the victim's body," Oresek replied. "Eddie is examining the scrapings under the microscope to determine if there's anything unexpected."

Eddie cleared his throat. "I've determined the scrapings are a mixture of cow manure, dirt, and hay. That's the same mixture we've recovered from the victim's clothing."

"Were there any surprises in the x-rays?" CJ asked.

Rolling his chair from the microscope to a computer, Eddie typed in a password, then moved the mouse. An x-ray image appeared on the computer monitor. "The victim had numerous healed broken bones. Here's her right humerus, and here's a healed break in her right ulna." Moving the mouse brought up a chest x-ray. "About half her ribs showed evidence of old fractures. Would you like to see more?"

As CJ shook her head, the M.E. said, "Unless she was involved in a terrible car accident at some time in the recent past, I'd say our victim suffered from a pattern of regular domestic abuse."

"Was there any alcohol in the victim's blood?"

Reading from a sheet of paper placed alongside the computer, Eddie replied, "Her blood alcohol was 0.11 percent." He looked up and added, "She was legally drunk. I didn't find any illegal drugs in her system."

Oresek stepped back from the examination table and watched CJ approach. "Under most circumstances, I'd say her intoxication was a contributing factor in her death."

"I take it this is not 'under most circumstances.'"

Oresek leaned over the victim's misshapen head, the left side crushed by the Bobcat. "I don't need to open the body to determine that the cause of death was massive head trauma. The bleeding indicates her heart was still beating when the Bobcat tire rolled over her head...the first time."

Carefully touching the victim's arm and head, Oresek traced a line across the victim's torso and head. "This was the first tire track." Indicating a second line, Oresek added, "And this is either the second or third track. At this point, the victim's heart had stopped."

CJ shook her head. Oresek nodded. "After examining the scene, I surmise she was crushed by three passes over her body. The first pass likely killed her."

"And the second and third were to make extra sure she wasn't getting up," CJ crossed her arms.

Eddie carried pictures of the Bobcat's position in the barnyard over to them. "I think the third pass was to position the Bobcat so it looked like she'd only been driven over once. The operator wasn't smart enough to realize the tires had left three sets of ruts in the muck."

"It was definitely murder," CJ said.

Oresek cocked his head. "It's hard to know what the Bobcat operator was thinking. If not for the contusion on the opposite side of the victim's head, the operator might argue the first pass was an accident. The other passes were to cover it up." Spreading the victim's hair on the undamaged part of her head, Oresek said, "It's hard to explain this antemortem bruise as anything other than an assault meant to disable the victim, followed by the skid steer attack to make it look like an accident."

Surprised by the news and disgusted by the long-term trauma suffered by the victim, CJ stepped back and considered the information. "The statutes define death while committing domestic abuse when the perpetrator has engaged in a past pattern of domestic abuse upon the victim, as first degree murder."

"Everything I've seen supports that conclusion." Oresek rolled over a tray covered with stainless steel instruments that looked suitable for a torture chamber. "I'm going to start my internal examination. Do you want to hang around to see what she had for breakfast, or do you have enough information?" Oresek asked.

"Since I'm here, I should watch the whole procedure."

"You can buy me lunch afterwards," Eddie joked.

After glancing at the victim's injuries again, CJ said, "I might be able to eat pancakes."

Although a surgical mask covered the M.E.'s mouth, the crinkled skin alongside his eyes revealed a smile. "What's the matter,

Sergeant? Haven't we toughened you up enough to face a steak after a postmortem?"

"I hope I'm never as callous as you and Eddie are."

As the M.E. made a Y-incision to access the victim's organs, he replied, "I have that same hope, for your sake."

* * *

After a lunch of pancakes and bacon, CJ considered her next steps in the Raster case. She settled into the afternoon drive down I-35. Spring meant the beginning of the road repair season. She prepared for merging with the other southbound drivers as the orange signs directed traffic to become a single lane.

The merger warning was irrelevant in the sparse traffic. More concerning was the car ahead of her who ignored the 55-mph work zone speed reduction and continued ahead at slightly over 70 mph. Noting the car's extreme speed on her radar, but unable to see the license plate number from her position, she called dispatch to report the vehicle's speed, description, and location. Trapped behind a car watching her in his mirror and going exactly 55 mph, she resigned herself to chasing the speeder down after clearing the construction zone.

In addition to his speed, the driver seemed to be weaving in the lane as if distracted or impaired. Seeing a work crew just ahead, CJ grimaced, hoping for the car to pass without incident. Although it was more than 200 yards ahead of her, she watched as it veered past the construction cones. A worker dressed in a lime green reflective vest was thrown away from the speeding vehicle after an impact.

"Dispatch, I need an ambulance and backup at mile marker 207 on southbound I-35. There's a vehicle/pedestrian accident in the work zone."

She activated her flashing lights causing the car ahead of her to veer onto the shoulder. She sped past that car toward the sudden string of brake lights approaching the scene of the accident. Other workmen rushed to the aid of the injured man. CJ noted that the speeding vehicle had pulled over a distance past the point of impact.

CJ blocked the lane, got out of her squad and rushed to the group of workmen gathered around the injured man. "I've got an ambulance on the way," she said, easing past the men, then kneeling next to the victim, whose leg was bent at an unnatural angle. "What's your name?"

"Nate," the man croaked.

"Okay, Nate, keep still. Help is on the way. Can you wiggle your fingers and toes for me?"

"Yeah, but my hip hurts like hell."

"You're banged up pretty badly. We'll get you into an ambulance as quickly as we can.

Okay?" She covered him with an emergency blanket from her squad to prevent shock.

"Sergeant?" A male voice behind CJ said. "Are you going to arrest that SOB who's probably talking to his lawyer right now?"

Glancing down the road at the driver standing outside of his black BMW, CJ nodded. "He's stopped. I'll deal with him in a minute after we're sure Nate is okay."

One of the workmen started walking toward the driver. Jogging to intercept him, CJ put a hand on his shoulder. "Hang on. I'll deal with him. Don't make this any worse."

"I'm going to put that idiot's teeth so far down his throat he'll have to chew steak with his asshole."

"Easy. You really don't want to do that. Go back to Nate and keep him comfortable until the ambulance arrives."

"That idiot was on his phone right up until he hit Nate. He didn't even realize anything was wrong until he heard the impact. Someone should take a baseball bat to that shiny car of his."

"The car will be impounded and he's going to the courthouse in the back seat of a squad car." The whine of a siren sounded in the distance. CJ glanced at the line of cars backed up behind her parked car. Noting two drivers who'd stopped immediately after the impact, she walked to the woman and teen who were standing next to their vehicles, patiently waiting to make their statements.

A third driver was kneeling next to Nate, assisting with his first aid. The dispatcher announced the two-minute ETA of the Moose Lake ambulance.

CJ's cell phone rang, the sound barely audible over the noise of the northbound traffic and wind. "This is CJ."

She was surprised to hear Eddie's voice. "Is that really you on live TV at an accident on I-35?"

"I'm at an accident scene." She looked around but didn't see the news crew or even anyone taking cellphone video.

"Look up."

CJ squinted as she looked up to the sky. "There's a drone overhead. Is it streaming this live?"

"Yeah. I'm watching Channel 10. They just cut into their afternoon news with this footage of an accident in a Pine County work zone."

"The ambulance is here, and I need to talk to the driver. See if they announce who's providing the drone feed. I'd like to get a copy of it."

* * *

After sending the injured worker away, CJ pointed out the driver of the BMW to a state trooper. "He was seventeen miles an hour over the work zone speed limit and weaving as if distracted. The workers reported that he was talking on the phone right up until he hit the victim."

"You witnessed the crash?"

"From a distance. I observed his erratic driving and noted his speed on my radar."

A slight grin spread across the trooper's face. "Well, that ought to stand up well in court."

"I told the other workers the BMW would be impounded in an effort to keep them from beating the shit out of that idiot," CJ grimaced.

"The tow truck is already on the way. I'll transport the driver to the courthouse after the car is towed," the trooper added.

"By the way, there was a drone taking video of the scene. We should try to track down the owner. I'm sure a jury would love to see that played out in a courtroom."

"That won't happen. Any defense attorney worth his retainer will petition to have that excluded as inflammatory. At a minimum, there will be a plea agreement before a jury ever sees that video." Both CJ and the Trooper knew that was the truth.

Chapter 7

CJ finished her freeway accident report, then walked up to the county attorney's office. She found her favorite assistant county attorney, Alissa, at her desk. She took a seat in her guest chair intending to share the latest information on the farm 'accident.'

"You look like you could use a drink or a good night's sleep, CJ."

"It's been a long day."

CJ told her about M.E.'s findings. "I think we have a first degree murder case against Craig Raster."

Sitting back, Alissa laced her fingers. "It sounds like murder after a long pattern of domestic abuse. That's murder one. For now, Tom has me drafting the complaint as we speak. You can sign the complaint warrant for second degree murder and go pick him up. Where do you think Mr. Raster is spending his day?"

"He's probably at his farmhouse drinking beer."

"Do you want to ruin his night, or do you want to arrest him tomorrow?"

Tipping her head back, CJ said, "I'd love to drag his butt in here right now. On the other hand, I'd like to go home and walk my dog before having a quiet dinner."

"If you don't think Raster is a flight or suicide risk, I'll finish the complaint warrant. You can pick him up in the morning."

* * *

As she drove home that night, thoughts of the Raster case distracted CJ, and she nearly hit a squirrel that darted across the road. A few miles east of town, she noticed a realtor's sign with an arrow pointing down a gravel road off County Road 10. Curious, she turned around and backtracked to the realty sign.

I haven't been down this road before, she thought as she passed two driveways opposite one another, each leading to a modest house with a small pole barn in back. The next driveways were a hundred yards farther down the road, indicating that each house was set on a five- or ten-acre lot. A white fence surrounded the place on the left where a grazing horse lifted his head as she passed.

Three strands of electric fence enclosed the right-hand lot. Part of the lot was weeds but also included a fenced pasture. The For Sale sign at the end of the driveway was less than fifty yards from the cul-de-sac which had three driveways leading into a wooded area.

Curious, CJ turned by the realty sign and followed the weedy driveway up to a concrete slab that ran from the house to the attached two-stall garage. Exiting her squad, she stared at the house in front of her. A sudden chill enveloped her as she realized it was eerily similar to a house she and her late husband, Bobby, were planning to buy a few years ago. Overcome with emotion, she clutched his silver St. Michael medal on a chain around her neck. Silent tears started to form in her eyes. So many broken dreams still sprung up on her when she least expected them. She brushed her cheeks as she walked the perimeter of the ranch-style home.

She counted the windows and estimated the house had three bedrooms and two baths. The garage was wide enough to park two cars or pickups, and long enough to store a lawn mower. A chain-link fence enclosed a small area behind the house. Inside the fence, a set of steps led to the rear door with a doggie flap cut into it.

There's a basset-sized dog door so Bailey can let herself in and out. Leaning her elbows on the fence, CJ studied the yard and house. The siding and trim were maintenance free. The neighbors were far enough away so they wouldn't be annoying. *I wonder what the house payments would be compared to my rent?*

Returning to her squad, CJ started the engine, then dialed the phone number on the realtor's sign. A message apologized for missing her call, then directed her to leave her name and number. "My name is CJ Jensen, and I'd like to talk to someone about the house that's for sale on the cul-de-sac off of County Road 10, east of Pine City."

A peaceful feeling came over CJ as she ended the call. The house seemed right for her. Driving toward the county road, a man rushed out of one of the houses, waving his arms. Rolling down the passenger window, she asked, "Can I help you?"

"I saw you pull into the driveway at Neilsens' place. Is everything okay?"

Smiling, CJ replied, "I saw the for sale sign and was checking out the house."

A look of relief swept the man's face. "That's good. We're a close-knit neighborhood and we watch out for each other. I'm Mike Gardner."

"It looks like the Neilsens moved out a while ago."

"They moved into the senior apartments in town for the winter. I talked to them a couple of weeks ago and they've decided this place is too much work for them, so they put it up for sale." Gardner paused, then asked, "You wouldn't know anyone who's interested, would you?"

"I might be interested, if I can swing the financing. I'm CJ Jensen."

A smile spread over Gardner's face. "I think everyone on the cul-de-sac would be pleased if a deputy moved in here. Where are you living now?"

"My basset hound and I live in an apartment in town."

"So, you're thinking about putting down roots?"

The thought of having roots in Pine County hadn't crossed CJ's mind, and the term startled her. "I've lived here for a couple of years now. I guess it might be time."

Gardner bent down and smiled. "The realtor is full of himself. He convinced the Neilsens he can get a lot more for this place than it's worth. If I call Bruce and Bev to tell them there's a nice deputy sheriff who's interested in their place, I'm certain they'd be willing to negotiate on the price. Especially if my wife and I put in a good word for you."

"I'm not sure that's entirely ethical."

"Sergeant Jensen..."

"Please call me CJ."

"Right. CJ, there's an old saying about not being able to pick your relatives but picking your neighbors. This is a *neighborhood*. Everyone here gets along and looks out for each other. In the summer, we get together and have cookouts. Marcy and I host a Christmas party. The Evans live at the end of the cul-de-sac, and they have a Kentucky Derby party. If you'd like to live here, I'll help make that happen."

"I don't know how you can make that offer."

"I'm the loan officer at the credit union. If you're making rent payments, have a steady job, and a decent credit rating, we can make this happen."

"Let's not get ahead of ourselves. I need to look at the interior and garage before I get too excited."

"The interior is practically worn out from all the cleaning. If you don't like the colors, we'll have a neighborhood painting party, and they'll change." Gardner looked over his shoulder at a woman who'd walked out of the house. "Marcy, come over here. Sergeant Jensen might be interested in Neilsens' place."

Marcy Gardner's cherubic face broke into a smile. "Sergeant?"

"I'm a sergeant with the sheriff's department, but please call me CJ."

"You might be interested in Neilsens' house?"

"I like the location and the lot. I need to see the interior."

Marcy elbowed her husband. "Give her the key."

"I can't..."

"We've had Neilsens' house key for years," Marcy explained. "It's time for us to walk through just to make sure the pipes haven't frozen, right dear?"

Gardner pulled a keyring from his pocket, removed a key and held it out to CJ. "I imagine you should take a look around to make sure no one has vandalized the place since I was in it last week."

Shaking her head, CJ smiled and held out her hand. "I'll just take a quick look around to make sure the door and windows are secure."

Gardner nodded. "You'd better make sure their John Deere lawn mower is still in the garage, too. I think they might be willing to include that in the sale."

"I'd appreciate it if you two would join me, just to make sure I don't steal or break anything."

Marcy nodded. "You drive on down there. We'll be a second behind you."

CJ walked into a kitchen with updated appliances. Standing on a mat by the door, she realized the floor was spotless. The living room to her right had carpeting with vacuum cleaner tracks. She slipped off her boots and walked down the hallway checking out the three bedrooms and a guest bathroom. The Gardners entered as she walked into the master bedroom and realized there was an en suite master bathroom with a walk-in closet.

Marcy walked up behind her and stood at the door. "What do you think?"

"Don't tell the realtor, but I love it. There's even a doggie door for my basset hound."

Marcy reached out and touched CJ's arm, a move that would normally have felt like an affront to her personal bubble, however, Marcy felt like a longtime friend. She whispered, "I can see you living here. Seriously. You belong here."

CJ nodded. "Let's see what the realtor says."

Marcy looked at her husband. "Make this happen, Mike."

"If this is the house you want, I'm pretty sure you'll be our new neighbor."

"I'm not much into partying," CJ said as she returned to the kitchen and put her boots on.

"We don't party," Marcy said. "We have family gatherings."

Mike Gardner nodded. "To be honest, we like our neighbors more than we like our relatives."

* * *

CJ entered the bullpen and noticed Pam was on the phone. When she finished, CJ let out a deep breath. Pam squinted at her and said, "Okay, what gives?"

"I think I might be buying a house."

"Um, how did you go from an autopsy to buying a house? Did Eddie decide it was time you two got a love nest?" She snickered.

"You've been dealing with Skunk Boy Riley today, so I'll let that comment slide. Who were you talking to, anyways?"

As Pam was about to answer her, CJ's cell phone rang. The Caller ID indicated it was the realtor.

"This is CJ," she answered nervously.

"Hi ya, you called about the house off 10? This is Casey Satter and that's my listing." The male voice came across as irritated instead of eager.

"Yes. I was wondering if you could give me more information. It looks perfect for me and my basset hound."

"You got a dog? What about a family? I'd be more than happy to talk to your husband about this place. Maybe he thinks you'll need something bigger," his arrogance amped up as he spoke.

"As I said, I am looking at this house and it appears to be exactly what my basset hound and I need," CJ felt her patience begin to fade. This Satter guy appeared to be an egotistical misogynist.

"Naw. I'll tell you what. I have a nice starter house listing for a single cat lady like yourself. It's in town. Something smaller and easier for you to manage on your own," Satter sneered.

"Mr. Satter? May I call you Mr. Satter?" CJ questioned through clenched teeth, "Can you give me more information on this listing, or do I need to speak with the head broker in your agency? It seems you may not be the right person with the information I need." Pam's eyes met CJ's across the desk. She smirked and mouthed, "Get 'im!"

"No, lady. I'm the man with the information. I am the premiere agent in Pine County. I have the freaking glass trophy in my office to prove it. Why don't you just get in your car and come down to my office. We'll see if we can find something that fits your needs," Satter snorted then rapidly fired off his office address. CJ grabbed a pen and caught the building number and street name before he abruptly hung up.

"How in the hell does that jackass tool bag sell houses with an attitude like that?" she asked Pam.

"No freaking clue. I bet he's got a cheek full of chew and oily hair," Pam responded. "Let's see what this asshole really looks like," she said as she pulled up Satter's realtor website. "Huh. I was right on the money. He's got oily hair, yellowish teeth and a whole lotta attitude. I guess this dude is super popular, too. Tons of one-star reviews. Hey, listen to this one," Pam began to read out loud while CJ simmered in her chair.

"Mr. Satter was never on time, never arrived when he said he would, nor did he offer any real assistance when buying our home," she snorted. "This one says he left their front door unlocked and their drawers in the kitchen were pulled open. Dirty shoe prints were left on the rug after he showed their home to a potential buyer. OH MY LORD. This one is the worst, CJ." Pam waved her hand emphatically to ensure her friend was listening. "Mr. Satter arrived at the showing, appeared to be INTOXICATED and told my wife to 'let us men handle this,' and to 'wait in the car.' I told him we would not be in need of his services and left immediately."

"Well, shit. This means I need to do a freaking background check on this ass in order to buy a house! I bet that last couple never reported him for DUI," CJ picked at a splint end on her ponytail, then flung it over her shoulder in disgust. "I just want to buy a house! Why is that so difficult?"

As CJ continued to rant, Pam piped in, "Hey, looks like he has two DUIs, one trespassing, one disorderly and a few parking tickets."

"Fantastic. I'm buying my house from a freaking criminal," CJ sighed. "Wish me luck. He doesn't have any outstanding warrants, does he?" She shook her head as Pam replied that he did not.

"Better get this over with as quickly as possible. This may be the one time I want to wear my uniform when I'm off duty," she groaned.

Pam leaned back in her chair and said, "I think you should contact Satter's real estate broker and arrange for someone else to act as your agent. Let that person deal with Satter."

CJ nodded as she let her irritation seep away. "That's a thought. Let someone else deal with the greasy asshole."

Pam turned to her computer and typed. "Barb Peterson is the broker in Satter's office. Give her a call and set up a house tour."

Distracted by her own internet search, CJ missed Pam's comment. "A broker?"

"Yes, Barb Peterson. Call her." Pam texted the phone number from the online ad.

Holding out her phone to Pam, she said, "Pull up MLS. There's a virtual tour of the house there."

They waited as the MLS tour of the home loaded. Pam clicked on the house picture taken from the street. "It's cute," she said as they waited for the other 26 images to load. Clicking through the pages, they saw the living room, kitchen, bedrooms, bathrooms, walk-in closet, and the entryway. Next came views of the garage, yard, and a small pole barn.

"Click on that 360 icon," CJ suggested.

Clicking on the icon brought them to an aerial video of the property. "This is great. There's drone footage of the house, yard, and neighborhood," Pam noted. "The houses are nicely separated for privacy, and the ones at the end of the cul-de-sac overlook a creek. The whole neighborhood looks lovely."

"The neighbors I met said they have potluck get-togethers that are like family gatherings." Smiling, CJ added, "It will be a great place to live."

"Don't tell Satter that! When you're with the realtor, act like you're lukewarm. Like it's something you might settle for, if pushed."

"I'll call the broker. She can be my buffer with Satter."

Pam's phone rang as CJ walked away. Seeing the caller ID from the county attorney's office, Pam smiled. "Hey, Alissa, do you have a signed warrant for me?"

"I do! Go arrest that abusive sonofabitch."

Pam smiled at the assistant county attorney's characterization of Craig Raster as Floyd walked into the bullpen and snorted. "Sure. Can you email the arrest warrant for the suspect?"

Alissa gasped. "Oh crap. Did someone else hear me say that?"

Laughing, Pam replied, "Floyd's here, and he feels the same way about the abusive sonofabitch."

Floyd put a pod into the coffee maker before commenting, "What sonofabitch do I dislike and who are you talking to?"

As she hung up the phone, Pam replied, "Alissa is emailing Craig Raster's arrest warrant to me."

Floyd watched the coffee dribble into his cup. "If you give me five minutes to finish my coffee, I'll ride along when you arrest the sonofabitch."

"No problem," Pam replied as she turned to her computer. "I'll print out the warrant and put on my vest."

The realty office receptionist answered CJ's call and asked her to hold. A few moments later, a woman answered, "This is Barb."

"I'm interested in a house you've got listed on Milkweed Lane."

The realtor's chair creaked as she shifted. "Hang on a second." A moment later, Peterson was back. "I've pulled it up. It's a lovely little three-bedroom rambler on five acres with an attached garage and pole barn."

"It looks like something I'd be interested in," CJ replied.

"Casey Satter is the listing agent. I can have him call you."

"Ms. Peterson, I'd be more comfortable dealing with you."

"Sure. No problem. When would it be convenient for you to tour the house?"

"I'm off-duty at three o'clock. Any time after that works."

The realtor's chair creaked again. "My calendar is clear at four-fifteen. I could meet you there, if that works for you."

"That would be perfect," CJ replied.

"I'll get the lock-box combination and meet you there."

Chapter 8

It took Craig Raster more than a minute to respond to Pam's knocks on his door. She pounded a second time and announced, "Sheriff's department."

Raster's bloodshot eyes and unshaven beard matched his rumpled shirt and jeans. "What do you want now?"

Pam pushed the screen door open and grabbed his right wrist and cuffed it. She put her hand on Raster's shoulder, spun him around and reached for his other wrist. "Craig Raster, you're under arrest for the murder of Donna Raster."

"First you take my Bobcat and now you go accusin' me of murdering that dumbass? How is it my freaking fault she's so stupid she stood behind the Bobcat? I couldn't see her well enough! How about it was an accident!" Craig Raster ranted and raved as Pam tried to put the cuff on his other wrist.

"Please put your hands behind your back so I can handcuff you," Pam calmly reiterated the order. Floyd watched as spittle and curse words flew out of Raster's mouth. "Mr. Raster, you have the right to remain silent. Anything you say CAN and WILL BE used against you in a court of law. You have the right to an attorney..." Pam continued as she finally clasped the last cuff and turned him around. Floyd stepped up to pat him down and they led him out to the waiting squad.

"Even the firemen told you what happened! It was an accident! Why are you arresting me?"

At this point, Raster had worked himself up into such a state Floyd was afraid they weren't going to be able to get him into the squad without physically helping him inside. He suspected Raster was either still heavily intoxicated or hung over from the previous evening's imbibing.

"Can you help me here, Mr. Raster? Pick your leg UP and SIT in the seat. I will put on your seatbelt for you." Pam instructed Craig as if she were playing a game of Simon Says with her young son. Raster turned and slurred in her face. She quickly held her breath as the distillery smell met her nose. Tugging at his pants to help seat him, Floyd asked, "Hey Craig, how much did you have to drink today?"

"Not much. Not any'ore 'an any other damn day! Why? Is it a crime to drink at home now? Y'all think an acc'dent is a crime now? I want my lawyer!" His last proclamation was met with a heavy load of spit, right in Pam's face.

CJ, who was late to the party, arrived in time to witness the spit shower. She pulled him away from Pam and said, "Mr. Raster, if you continue to spit in the face of my deputy, we will charge you with assault. Please contain your bodily fluids!"

Pam hooked his seatbelt as CJ grabbed some tissues for Pam to clean herself. CJ whispered to Floyd and Pam out of Raster's earshot, "Well, we damn well know that vermin hasn't had his shots. I hope you don't catch anything from him." She nudged Pam with her elbow as Floyd suppressed a smile.

"I'll take him in and book him. Don't worry. I'll wear my face shield." Pam rolled her eyes and grunted.

* * *

Later that afternoon, CJ and Pam were in the bullpen when the sheriff walked in carrying his coffee cup. Nodding to the sheriff, CJ whispered, "Don't say anything about the Raster case. I don't need John's input on which wild hares we could be chasing."

Pam smiled and nodded as the sheriff walked over. "You two look like you're conspiring on something. Are you making headway on the Raster case?"

CJ smiled. "He's in custody."

"Okay." Frowning as his mind changed direction, the sheriff asked, "Who have you got scheduled for the Hinckley Corn and Clover Days parade?"

"Riley and Kerm will be there, not that we're expecting any trouble."

After a moment of consideration as the coffee maker sputtered, the sheriff's face brightened. "You know that I'm planning to walk in the parade, right?"

CJ nodded. "I figured you would. It is an election year."

"Why don't you walk with me? Your face is recognizable and it's nice to show the department's diversity."

CJ quickly turned to Pam. "I think it would be better to have Pam walk with you. You'd be showing diversity and youth!"

Pam's sly smile prefaced her reply, "No, I think CJ should be the one in the parade, and she should bring Bailey, wearing her Pine County Sheriff's Department K9 vest."

The sheriff's face brightened. "That would be perfect! The kids would love having a dog with us. Plan on it."

The sheriff walked to the coffee machine as CJ glared at Pam. She hissed, "I will get you back for that."

Pam, grinning ear to ear, replied, "I doubt you'll be able to equal that."

The sheriff paused in the hallway before returning to his office. "I think the parade starts at ten o'clock. We'll need to be lined up half an hour early." He looked like he was ready to leave, but added, "You know, Isanti County has their sheriff's mounted posse ride in the local parades and work crowd control at the fair and rodeo. We should think about something like that."

Pam rolled her eyes as the sheriff walked away and whispered, "Yeah, then someone needs to walk behind them to shovel the road apples."

"Noah might have a good time picking up road apples," CJ said as she stepped away.

"Not funny," Pam replied to CJ's back.

* * *

At the end of her shift, CJ picked up Bailey and changed into jeans and a t-shirt. After a short walk, she unclipped Bailey's leash inside the apartment. The dog immediately hopped onto the couch and groaned as she settled there.

"Here's the deal. I'm going to look at a house where you could run in the yard. You're going to behave yourself while I'm gone. Okay?"

Bailey listened, then farted before closing her eyes.

"Fine. I'm glad you agree."

Turning onto Milkweed Lane, CJ saw a cream-colored Cadillac parked in the house's driveway. Mike Gardner looked up from the bushes he was pruning, apparently checking to see who was driving down the road. CJ waved, causing Mike to smile and nod to her.

After parking alongside the Caddy, CJ walked to the back door, which opened as she prepared to knock. "You must be CJ?" a trim middle-aged woman asked as she held the door open.

"I am. And you must be Barb Peterson."

Stepping aside, the realtor handed CJ a printout with the house information before closing the door behind them. "I toured this place when Casey first listed it, and I'd forgotten how cute it was."

Pretending it was her first time inside the house, CJ scanned the printout, looked around the kitchen, and into the living room. "This is nice. How long has the house been on the market?"

Gesturing toward the empty living room, Barb replied, "It's been on the market for two months. Casey has had a few showings. He said most people were looking for either more or less acreage. It's in that niche where it's not quite a hobby farm and is more to mow than a lot of people want."

"It has its own well and septic system?"

"Right," Barb replied. "That's another strike against it for anyone who's accustomed to city living. On the other hand, there's tranquility that you can't get in town."

CJ walked down the hallway into the master bedroom. "I like the quiet. I've been living in an apartment and I'm ready to not have a neighbor on the other side of the wall."

"Because the road ends in a cul-de-sac, there's very little traffic other than the few neighbors who live down the road." Noting the dog hair on CJ's jeans, the realtor added, "And there's a fenced yard for pets."

Chuckling, CJ walked to the other bedrooms. "You should've been a detective, Barb. You saw the dog's hair."

When she smiled, the crow's feet showed at the corners of the realtor's eyes. "We learn to read our customers."

"The carpeting is a little worn," CJ said, noting the only flaw she'd seen.

"I'm sure the sellers know that and would be flexible in their price if you felt it needed to be replaced." Reading CJ's interest, Barb added, "We have a good relationship with the bank's mortgage broker if you'd like to see what payments would be."

"What are the property taxes?"

"It's in the Pine City school district and the Pine County sheriff's department provides police protection. The taxes are on the second page of the handout." The realtor paused to allow CJ to read. "Is there a specific reason you didn't want to deal with Casey?"

"I spoke with him, then read his online reviews. Is he always...politically incorrect with his customers?"

The realtor's smile faded as she composed her response. "Casey has his strengths."

"Dealing with women isn't among them."

"He puts together wonderful marketing packages and many of his sellers have loved the service he provides. Did you look at the aerial tour of the property? No one else offers that."

"You're Casey's broker, but you could also act as the buyer's realtor, right?"

"Um, certainly. If you make an offer, we'll sign a contract specifying that I'm your agent, with fiduciary responsibility to act in your best interest."

"With the current mortgage rates, I can afford the house if we offer thirty thousand less than the asking price. Will you draw up a purchase agreement for that?"

Apparently surprised by the question, the realtor paused. "We can certainly *offer* that. I think you should expect the sellers to counteroffer."

"Let's write it up."

"You haven't seen the garage or the barn."

"I looked at Casey's photo montage and video. I'm comfortable offering based on what I've seen."

"Don't you want to talk to the bank first?"

CJ smiled. "The payments aren't much more than my rent. Let's write it up."

The realtor checked her watch. "I'll work on it tonight. Do you want to be listed by the initials CJ on the contract, or by your full name?"

Sighing, CJ replied, "My legal name is Charlene Joy Jensen."

The realtor nodded. "That's what I'll use on the contract. Can you come by the office tomorrow morning to sign the offer?"

CJ nodded. "Will ten o'clock work? Can Casey present the offer and have a response by five?"

The realtor seemed flustered as she closed and locked the door. "Certainly. We can do that. The sellers might be more motivated if you provided a mortgage pre-approval letter with the offer."

"No problem. I'll talk to the credit union mortgage guy first thing in the morning."

As they walked to the driveway, the realtor asked, "Do you have a family, CJ?"

"It's just me and the dog."

"Where do you work?"

CJ paused, then said, "I'm a Pine County employee. I have great benefits and job security."

The realtor stopped with her hand on the car door. "Okay. I'll write up an offer and see you in the morning."

Pausing by the realtor's car, CJ nodded. "Great. I'll take a quick walk around the property."

Mike Gardner was still working on his bushes when CJ parked in the road. He pulled off his gloves and set them on top of the brush pile he'd made before walking to meet her in the driveway. "You're back for another look."

CJ laughed. "I came back for an *official* tour of the house. I told the realtor to write up an offer."

Smiling broadly, Mike offered his hand. "I'll call Neilsens and tell them we've met our new neighbor."

"Let's not get ahead of ourselves," CJ replied, also smiling. "They may not accept my offer."

Gardner's smile turned mischievous. "I think they might be swayed by input from one of their old friends."

"Let's hope that's true, and let's hope the credit union thinks I'm a good mortgage risk."

Chapter 9

The next day, Pam's trip to the BCA in St. Paul was slowed by road construction in Forest Lake. *I can't believe all these people make this commute every day,* she thought as the traffic crawled through the construction zone.

After parking in a fenced lot alongside the brick building housing the Minnesota Bureau of Criminal Apprehension's headquarters, Pam walked to the receptionist's window, which was obviously made of bulletproof glass. She unfolded the case with her badge and Pine County ID, then slipped them through a pass-through. She consulted her phone for her BCA contact's name. "I'm here to see Brett Collins."

The receptionist smiled and checked Pam's ID, then passed it back. "I'll let Agent Collins know you're here. Please take a seat."

The lobby resembled what Pam expected to see when visiting a major corporation. Couches and chairs were arranged into clusters, each with a table. The walls were adorned with paintings and photos of Minnesota scenery, and there were potted birch trees in two of the corners. She sat in the nearest chair and paged through email on her phone until she heard the electronic click of the lock on a door next to the receptionist.

Brett Collins was about twenty-five, gangly, and dressed in a polo shirt with a BCA logo and dress pants. If not for the gun and badge on his belt, he could have been mistaken for a computer nerd. Pam introduced herself and was guided into a hallway.

"Your skid steer is in the garage. I apologize for the long walk."

"No problem," Pam replied. "I've been in the car for over an hour. I need to get some steps in."

"I looked at a map after we spoke. To be honest, I didn't know where Pine County was until this morning."

"It's a hundred miles north and a totally different world."

"There appear to be a lot of lakes, swamps, state forests, and a gigantic state park."

"Yes, we joke that it's 1,400 square miles, most of which is under a lake or swamp. The population doubles during the summer due to the tourists from the city."

They stopped at an elevator and Collins pushed the down button. "Wow, 1,400 square miles. Do you have like two hundred deputies to cover that much area 24/7?"

Pam laughed as they stepped into the elevator. "Our department is 74 people including jailers and bailiffs."

Collins stared at her. "Seriously?"

"Yes."

"What is your response time to an emergency call?"

They stepped into a hallway and Collins gestured to the right.

"It depends on where the deputies are patrolling. It can be anywhere from a few minutes to nearly an hour."

"An hour?"

"That's exaggerating. If we're too far away, we get an agency assist from the neighboring county and the state patrol."

Using a key card, Collins unlocked the door to a cavernous garage. In addition to the Bobcat, there were a number of other vehicles. In the center was a Mercedes SUV being totally dismantled.

"What's with the Mercedes?" Pam asked.

"It's full of drugs. We've pulled bags of powder and pills out of every nook and cranny." A technician dressed in white coveralls was operating a tire mounting machine. It whined as an arm pulled the tire away from the metal rim. When it stopped, the technician reached his gloved hand inside the tire and pulled out a brick of white powder. Holding it up, he smiled at Collins. "Even the tires are packed!"

Collins handed Pam a pair of purple gloves as they approached the Bobcat. A pair of legs wearing white coveralls stuck out from under the back of the skid steer.

"Hey, Brian. Investigator Ryan is here about the Bobcat."

A trim technician with a touch of gray at his temples, squirmed out from under the Bobcat. Standing, he pulled off rubber gloves and offered his hand. "I'm Brian Moorcroft. I didn't think anyone from Pine County would be here until later."

"Pam Ryan. I drove down first thing this morning. Brett said you guys had time to look at the Bobcat today."

Patting the orange counterweight on the back of the Bobcat, Brian nodded. "I just checked the hydraulics. Everything seems to be connected properly and is intact. What else did you want to know?"

"Is there some way the Bobcat could've backed up without someone actually moving the controls?"

"It's difficult to do anything accidentally with a skid steer. The engineers designed them so they're relatively idiot-proof. They have lots of safety features and all the controls default to stop when they're released."

Pam gestured toward the Bobcat's cab. "It's been a while since I've operated our John Deere skid steer on the farm. Can you show me how the Bobcat works?"

Brian climbed into the cab, fastened the seatbelt and lowered the safety bar that held the driver in place. "That's the first safety feature. It won't start unless the operator has lowered the safety bar to secure himself in the seat." He reached up to the upper right corner of the cab and turned a key that started the noisy engine. After checking the area around him, Brian lifted his hands and said, "Nothing happens if you don't have your hands on the controls."

"The left handle is the directional control?" Pam asked, knowing the answer.

Nodding, Brian turned his head to ensure no one was standing near him. "There's no one behind me, right?"

Pam glanced behind the Bobcat and shook her head. "It's clear."

Brian pulled back on the left control handle slightly. The Bobcat moved backward. He released the handle and it stopped. Pushing the handle forward made the Bobcat move ahead. It stopped when he let go of the controls.

Pam raised her voice to be heard over the engine. "There's no way for the machine to back up without moving that control handle, right?"

Brian shook his head. "The left handle controls the tires. The right handle controls the bucket." He pulled back on the other control handle in his right hand, raising the bucket. Pushing it to the side tipped the bucket. Pushing the other direction, dumped it. Centering the control, he leveled, then lowered the bucket to the ground. "Neither the tires nor the bucket move without pushing the controls. Everything stops when you take your hands away."

"Could you see someone behind the Bobcat?"

Brian shut off the engine, then twisted in the seat, looking back. "No, not really. That's the biggest safety flaw."

Envisioning Donna Raster's position, Pam said, "Speculate on how an operator would accidentally back over someone."

Brian climbed out of the cab and stood alongside the Bobcat. "It could happen if the operator was in a hurry and didn't look behind himself."

"That would be negligent."

Brian nodded. "That would be plain stupid. Anyone who runs a skid steer knows you check behind it before you turn the key."

"Okay, let's say that stupid accident happened. The operator backed over someone. How would he pull ahead and run over the victim again?"

Initially speechless, Brian shrugged and said, "I suppose he might've panicked and pushed the controls."

Pam nodded, careful not to bias the technician's comments. "Suppose he panicked and ran over her a second time as he pulled ahead. After that, he reversed and backed over the victim again. How would that happen?"

Brian frowned and silently considered the question. "I can't envision any way that could happen accidentally."

"If you were called as a witness, what would you say about this machine's mechanical condition and the chance it backed over the victim due to a malfunction?"

"It's an older machine, but the mechanics are good. The controls work as they're supposed to. It didn't back up by accident. The operator must've had his hand on the controls."

"What's your professional opinion about the operator's claim that he ran back and forth over the victim three times without knowing he'd struck her?"

"First of all, I expect the victim would've stepped aside or would have warned the operator they were behind him. Second, the machine would've rocked as the tires ran over the victim's body—the operator would've felt that. Third, we found blood on the bucket. It's hard to believe the operator didn't notice the victim's body alongside the bucket before he backed over the victim a second time."

Pam thanked the technician and turned to Collins as she stripped off her gloves. "I guess that's what I needed to know. The machine is intact and functioning as designed. There's no chance there was a mechanical malfunction that caused the death."

Collins led Pam out of the garage and back to the elevator. "I'm a mechanical engineer, and I reviewed the design specifications and operating manual. That machine functions properly. You're dealing with operator malfeasance or a deliberate act."

"At best, criminal negligence. At worst, homicide," Pam said as they entered the elevator.

Collins nodded. "I'd be comfortable testifying to that.

"How did an engineer end up in the BCA?" Pam asked. "I thought everyone here was a cop or lawyer."

"We've got a variety of scientists, from analytical chemists to a limnologist."

"What's a limnologist?" Pam asked as they returned to the lobby.

"They're scientists who specialize in freshwater biology. We have a number of crimes that have been solved by analyzing lake and river water samples for their chemistry and microbes."

"That's amazing."

Collins held the lobby door open as they exited the hallway. "It's an interesting place to work. Every case is different."

Chapter 10

Sawyer Larson stood in the waiting room of the Pine County Attorney's Office and tugged at his light blue tie. He had successfully navigated the stairs without spilling the contents of his briefcase. He smoothed over his thinning crown as he waited patiently for the receptionist to notice him through her security window. His tan suit was rumpled, and his shoes needed a good polish, but the newest Pine County public defender was proud of his accomplishments, including the fact he had just been handed what could turn out to be the largest, most public murder case of his short career.

"Uh, ma'am?" Sawyer quietly knocked on the glass partition. He tugged at his tie once again and scratched his Adam's apple. The receptionist appeared not to have heard him. He pulled himself up to his full height of five feet, nine inches, summoned the strength his Me-Maw said he had inside, and tapped louder.

"Ma'am!" Sawyer's slightly elevated voice attracted the attention of the middle-aged, mousy brown-haired receptionist who gave him the once over and suppressed a snort, thinking his suit looked like it belonged to his shorter and heavier father.

"Can you tell me why you're here, young man?" She took in the image of the boy-man standing before her and tried her hardest not to laugh. He was turning as red as his hair and resembled a taller version of her grandson playing dress up.

"Uh, I'm here to see the county attorney...er, uh Tom B-B-Bakken," he stuttered out the name as he wrestled with his anxiety. "I, uh, am the new public defender, Sawyer Larson. Maybe you've heard of me?" The receptionist decided Larson was a puppy who had retrieved a stick and dropped it at her feet, waiting for a pat on the head.

"I will tell Mr. Bakken that you're here. Have a seat." She motioned to the utilitarian chairs the county provided their office for waiting visitors.

Ten minutes later, Tom Bakken appeared at the door and held it open for Sawyer as he stuck out his hand to introduce himself. "Tom Bakken."

"Sawyer Larson. Maybe you've heard of me? Mr. B-B-Bakken?" His childlike hopeful tone was not lost on the senior attorney. Tom motioned for the eager public defender to follow him down the long hallway to his corner office.

"You must be Raster's public defender. Welcome to Pine County," Tom flashed his politician smile and motioned for the young man to have a seat in one of the two chairs in front of his wide oak desk. Tom chuckled to himself as he took his seat behind the desk and gave the public defender the once over. He knew exactly why Mr. Larson was gracing his office with his presence, yet he waited for the young man to open the conversation.

"I, uh, yeah. Thanks." Sawyer began to scratch his Adam's apple as he set his briefcase at his feet. He wasn't exactly sure how he wanted to begin the conversation. "I, uh, am here, sir, b-b-because..."

Sawyer's face began to color, and his scratching became more intense as Bakken took pity on him and interrupted, "It's okay. Call me Tom. Would you like something to drink? Water? Coffee?"

The young attorney looked up from his lap and nodded his head vigorously and squeaked out, "Water, please."

Tom leaned over to his mini fridge, grabbed a bottle of cold water and handed it to Sawyer. He waited a beat while the young lawyer took a long drink, then found his voice.

"I, uh, am Mr. Raster's attorney, sir. And I'm here to talk about making a deal," He crossed his legs, bumped his water bottle, then abruptly uncrossed them when he realized he had dumped half of the water in his lap.

"AAAAAAAAHHHHHHHH!" Larson jumped out of his chair to escape the puddle forming on the seat.

Tom grabbed a few tissues and handed them across his desk to the now hopping attorney. "Here, let me grab a few paper towels for you," Tom said. Then he disappeared into the adjoining bathroom and reappeared with a handful of paper towels. Larson continued to dance around as he wiped up the wet chair and dabbed at the wet crotch of his trousers. Tom suppressed a smile. He hoped that the young attorney didn't have anywhere else to go other than home after this meeting.

Finally settling down to business after tossing the soaked towels in the trash, Sawyer stared expectantly at Bakken.

"So, how 'bout it?"

"So, how about what, Mr. Larson?" Bakken had all but given up on a serious conversation at this point in their meeting. He held empathy for this bumbling youngster, yet didn't want to show his hand. That being the fact that he had contemplated offering a second degree murder charge in exchange for Larson's client's guilty plea. The sheriff's department hadn't brought enough proof for a first degree charge as yet, although the M.E. had provided them with the autopsy report showing previously healed broken bones, indicating past domestic violence perpetrated by the defendant on the victim.

"A deal?" Larson stuttered. He had just begun to compose himself after his water bottle debacle.

"What kind of deal?" Bakken asked.

"Uh, manslaughter. Second degree."

"Mr. Larson, I don't think that is appropriate for this case," Bakken crossed his hands on his desk.

"Uh, yes, Minnesota State Statute reads, 'A person who causes the death of another by any of the following means is guilty of manslaughter in the second degree and may be sentenced to imprisonment for not more than ten years or to payment of a fine of not more than $20,000, or both: (1) by the person's culpable negligence whereby the person creates an unreasonable risk, and consciously takes chances of causing death or great bodily harm to another.'"

Sawyer sat back in his chair, signaling he was done. Tom Bakken bit his lip and sighed. The kid could memorize statutes, that was for certain. However, he really was living in a dream world if he thought his client was simply negligent.

"Well, Mr. Larson, I will take your offer under advisement. Please look for my offer letter in the mail in the next few days. Now, I know you'll want to address the issue of your trousers before your next appointment, so I don't want to keep you from taking care of necessary personal business." Tom stood and held out his hand to shake, hoping that Sawyer would take the hint that the meeting was over and that he needed to change his soaking wet pants.

Later that afternoon, after a quick change of pants and a tuna fish sandwich prepared by his mother, Sawyer Larson stood stock still in front of the heavy metal door of the jail. He clutched his briefcase to his chest and dabbed at the mayo stain on his tie. The jailer nodded him through security and searched his briefcase, then showed him to a small room where he sat in a chair and waited for his client.

Craig Raster, clad in an orange jumpsuit and black slides, shuffled into the room scowling. His gray hair was matted to his head as if it hadn't seen a brush in days.

"Yeah, what the hell do you want?" Craig dropped his medium-sized frame into the metal chair across the small table from his squirming red-haired lawyer.

"I, uh, am your public defender," Larson stuttered. "You know, the person the judge appointed the other day at your arraignment?" Sawyer busied himself with placing his briefcase on the table and removing a legal pad from it. He subconsciously twirled his pen between his fingers in a nervous twitch.

"The hell I need one of you dumbasses in a suit for? It was a freaking accident and nobody 'round here seems to have the sense God gave a goose. If you're my lawyer, ya need to get me the hell outta here. I haven't had a drink in DAAAAAYS." Raster punctuated his final words with a finger pointed directly at Larson's nose. He sputtered and ran his fingers through his gray hair and glared at the younger man.

"I, uh, talked to Mr. B-B-Bakken, sir. We, uh, are in the middle of negotiations. We can get a deal made, sir. A real good one, too. You won't have to do much prison time at all," Sawyer smiled feebly at his client, mustering up all his courage.

"I SAID, GET ME THE HELL OUT OF HERE, YOU SNOT-NOSED BRAT! WHAT PART OF THAT DON'T YOU AND YOUR FANCY DEGREE UNDERSTAND?" Raster jumped up from his chair and pounded his cuffed fists on the table in front of them. Sawyer jumped so high he knocked his chair over. The jailer appeared when he heard the commotion and asked if everything was okay.

"Yeah, uh, sure. We're discussing my client's case. I, uh, am providing for his best defense in this matter," Sawyer waved off the jailer and took his seat. Raster was still glaring at Sawyer as he proceeded to replace all of his office supplies in his briefcase. He nodded to his client and simply stated, "Mr. Raster, one hundred thousand dollars is quite a bit of money. If you have it lying around somewhere, I can post it for your bail and you can be back at your farm before sunset. If you do not, I suggest you work on the sudoku puzzles I've left for you with the jailers to help pass the time. I am working diligently on your defense and will be in touch after I receive the offer letter from Mr. B-B-Bakken. Thank you very much for your time," Sawyer Larson walked to the door, rapped lightly and left once the jailer appeared. His client, open-mouthed, sat silently gazing after his stuttering milquetoast lawyer.

* * *

CJ met Riley at the Sandstone sheriff's substation. "Here's the non-emergency number for the fire department. Leave a message for the chief saying you're interested in becoming a volunteer fireman."

Riley fingered the note with the phone number. "I'm not sure this is a good idea. I'm not really interested in becoming a volunteer fireman."

"This is an undercover assignment."

Glancing at CJ then back to the phone number, he said, "Wouldn't someone like Deputy Maki be a better choice? He's got a lot more experience."

"Riley, you're perfect for this," CJ said, trying to sell it.

"How am I perfect? You've already said I'm green."

"This will give you lots of experience. You'll hone your acting skills while gathering intelligence about what Craig Raster may have told his fireman buddies about killing his wife."

"How am I going to do that?"

"Attend their meetings and go to the bar with the guys afterwards. Schmooze them. Get them to open up to you about their lives and secrets."

"*Schmooze*? What does that even mean?"

"Butter them up. Make them feel important, like they're the experts. They'll want to teach you about things. Once they warm up to you, they'll start telling stories. Don't bring up Raster immediately. Let them tell you whatever stories they want to tell. Once they trust you, ask about their lives, where they live, what's going on in the department, then casually ask about Raster and the comments he's made about his wife."

"Will I have to drink beer?"

Growing impatient and questioning her choice of Riley as the best person to go undercover with the firemen, CJ sucked air in through her nose and said, "It'd be okay to sip a beer slowly, or go to the bar and order soda water with a lime. That looks like a gin and tonic. Whatever you do, don't get drunk, and don't drive if you are drinking alcohol." After pausing, CJ suggested, "Tell them you have to work the night shift and can't drink. Stick with Coke or Diet Coke."

"I don't like Coke."

Exasperated, CJ threw up her hands, "Fine, have iced tea. Order a root beer. What you're drinking doesn't matter. As long as they're drinking, they'll relax and share things that wouldn't come out when they're sober."

"If I see one of them getting drunk and driving away, should I pull him over?"

Grimacing, CJ asked, "Don't you think that would blow your cover?"

Riley processed that. "Is that a rhetorical question?"

"Yes, it is. Don't pull anyone over. Call 911 discreetly from the bathroom or outside."

Riley nodded but didn't say anything.

Preparing to move from suggesting to ordering, CJ allowed him to ponder his next argument or question.

Riley stared at the slip of paper for a moment, then said, "I'll call. Do you think they'll actually accept me?"

"The chief told me they're always recruiting. They never have enough firemen."

Bobbing his head, Riley said, "I'll leave a message. I'll let you know what the chief says."

CJ patted his shoulder and said, "Good plan." In her squad, CJ sat quietly, while mulling their conversation. *Have I set him up to fail? Will they kill him by sending him into a burning building?*

Shifting her squad into gear, CJ pulled out of the parking lot and drove through the few blocks of downtown Sandstone, then turned north onto Highway 23.

* * *

Pam placed another call to the Duluth television station, attempting to determine who had given them the video of the car accident on the freeway. She'd left a message for the station manager the first time and never received a reply. Deciding to take a different approach, she asked for the news producer.

After a few minutes on hold, her call was answered by a young woman. "Hello? This is Fallon Harris."

"Hi, Ms. Harris. I'm Pam Ryan, an investigator from the Pine County Sheriff's Department. We're investigating an accident on I-35 that occurred a couple of days ago involving a BMW. Your station aired drone coverage from the accident scene. We'd like to get the original, unedited drone footage to assist with our investigation."

"Um, I'm not sure what our policy is regarding the release of video footage that's given to us."

"Your news broadcasts are copyrighted, correct?"

"Um, yeah. I think so."

"Since it's copyrighted, you can at least provide me with a copy of your broadcast."

"Okay..."

Pam gave the producer her email address. "Please send me a copy of that segment of your broadcast."

"I'll figure out how to do that. Is that all you need?"

Pam hoped for the best when asking the next question. "I'd like the name of the person who sent you the footage, so we can get the full uncut video."

"I'm not sure I can..."

"Didn't you run a ribbon with the name of the source when you showed the video?"

"I really don't..."

"Fallon, don't you always credit people when you show their video?"

"I guess we do. Sure."

"Who sent you that video?"

"Hang on."

Pam waited as elevator music played over the phone. *I hope this works.*

"Investigator Ryan? Are you still there?"

"Yes."

"I spoke with the executive producer. He said I can release the source's name to you. Hang on for a minute while I look up the videographer's name." The line went silent for over two minutes, then Fallon said, "Here it is. That video was supplied by Casey Satter, who told us he lives in Pine City."

Shocked, Pam hesitated.

"Ms. Ryan, are you there?"

"Yes. Yes. I'm just noting the name."

"Do you still want me to send you the segment we aired?"

"Yes, please. It may take me a while to reach Mr. Satter. Thank you."

"No problem. Um, Ms. Ryan?"

"Yes?"

"I'm relatively new here. Could I use you as a contact? The boss suggested I develop contacts in the local communities, and I really don't know anyone in Pine County."

"I'm not the spokesperson for the department. You should talk to Sheriff Sepanen."

"I'd prefer to speak with someone…normal. You know, not a big shot. Do you understand?"

Smiling, Pam pictured a young woman who'd just started her first job. "Sure. You can call me any time. I may not be able to comment on some cases."

"Fair enough. Thank you!" The producer paused, then asked, "Can you tell me anything about the farm accident in Hinckley? That's in your county, right?"

A light bulb went off in Pam's head as Fallon spoke. Marvel Erickson had mentioned hearing a "buzzing." Pam quickly pulled her thoughts back to the conversation. "Yes, that farm death was in Pine County. We're investigating it now."

"Was it an accident?"

Carefully weighing her words, Pam said, "The Medical Examiner determined that the incident was not an accident."

"Not an accident? What does that mean?"

"We've arrested the victim's husband."

"No shit!" Realizing she'd made an unprofessional statement, Fallon said, "I'm sorry. Geez, that's...big news. Can I attribute that information to you?"

Chuckling, Pam said, "Most news outlets want confirmation from two sources before they report anything. I suggest you call the sheriff, John Sepanen, and ask him that question. You'll be able to quote him."

"Wow! Thank you, Ms. Ryan."

"Call me any time, Fallon. I'll tell you what I can."

Chapter 11

With his fingers steepled as he sat deep in thought, Floyd contemplated the Raster murder case while staring out his office window. A knock on the door frame interrupted his concentration. He was surprised to find County Commissioner Will Stark standing at his door. "We've got a problem," Will said as he closed Floyd's office door.

"What problem do we have?"

Stark sat himself in Floyd's guest chair, uninvited. "I'm being blackmailed."

"What?"

Will pulled a crumpled sheet of paper from his pocket and tossed it onto Floyd's desk. Unwilling to accept the commissioner's obvious attempt to manipulate him into unfolding the paper and responding to the alleged crime, Floyd glanced at the wadded paper and said, "I'll ask Pam Ryan to look into it in a bit. Right now, she's tied up in the Raster murder investigation."

Stark leaned forward, unable to believe Floyd would take his personal situation so casually. "I expect *you* to investigate this. It's a delicate matter."

"Pam is a professional. I assure you she'll handle the matter with the utmost discretion. Of course, if your blackmailer is arrested, we'll have to involve the county attorney and eventually, the matter WILL become public."

Will sniffled and leaned back. "I think we can deal with this outside of the court system."

"Who is your blackmailer, Will?"

"If I knew that, I wouldn't be here."

"Oh, so you want us to identify your blackmailer *and* stop them. ALL without involving the county attorney or the courts?"

"Yes."

"Why wouldn't you want the county attorney involved? Extortion is a felony."

Sniffling again, Will replied, "It's a delicate situation."

Intrigued, Floyd cocked his head. "Involving something you'd rather not have publicized."

"I'm relying on your discretion."

"Why are you asking *me* to investigate?" Floyd paused, then smiled. "Let me guess. The sheriff is elected and not subject to your whims. The deputies are civil servants who are protected by their union. I'm an 'at will' appointee, who can be dismissed by a vote of the county commissioners."

Stark squirmed in the chair. "I'd hoped you'd be the most discreet person."

"So, what's this about, Will?"

"Blackmail."

"I got that. *Why* are you being blackmailed?"

The commissioner shook his head. "That's irrelevant. I just want to identify the blackmailer and make it clear to him that it has to end."

"Or?" Floyd asked.

"Or, what?"

"What's my leverage if I can't threaten to arrest and charge him?"

"Well...you can threaten to charge him. Just don't do it when he agrees to stop."

Clenching his eyes shut and scratching his head, Floyd asked, "Why are you being blackmailed? An affair? Gambling? What?"

Stark stared at his hands. "I'm not sure it's..."

"What's on the paper you've crumpled up?"

"It's an email demanding money."

"If you don't pay the blackmailer, what's going to happen?"

"He's going to reveal something."

Floyd leaned his elbows on his desk. "If you want me to deal with whatever this is, you'll have to tell me what's going on."

Stark drew a breath and blew it out. "I'm raising puppies."

"Okay. What's the big secret? Do you have a dog fighting ring or are you abusing them?"

Stark shook his head emphatically. "None of that. I'm just raising and selling puppies."

Leaning back, Floyd asked, "Why are you being blackmailed? There's nothing illegal or immoral about raising puppies."

"There might be a few more dogs than people think I should have."

"How many?"

"I'm not entirely sure."

"More than five, ten, twenty?"

"I think we sold about two hundred last year. I specialize in French bulldogs and Shih Tzus."

"Two hundred? Seriously?"

Stark nodded.

"What's the issue? Are you not paying sales tax on the sales, or what?" When Stark didn't immediately respond Floyd asked, "Income tax?"

"I haven't got a kennel license and I'm not sure about the tax situation."

"Christ on a cracker, Will! You're a damn county official operating an illegal puppy mill and you're unsure of your tax situation?"

Stark checked the door and motioned for Floyd to lower his voice. "I'll get a license and talk to my accountant. I need you to keep this quiet and make this blackmailer go away."

Nodding toward the wadded paper, Floyd asked, "How much is the blackmailer asking?"

"Twenty thousand by Friday."

"How are you supposed to deliver the money?"

"He's going to let me know."

"You have no idea who the blackmailer is?"

Will glared at Floyd. "Do you think I'd be sitting here if I knew who was doing this? I'd..."

"You'd what?"

"I'd take care of him myself."

"That sounds illegal."

Stark threw up his hands. "What he's doing is illegal."

"But revenge is also illegal. You would be arrested if you did something illegal."

Stark smirked. "Not in this county."

Floyd leaned over his desk. "Especially in this county. I will arrest you and help the county attorney draft the complaint."

"John will step in."

Floyd shook his head. "The sheriff is a law enforcement officer who took an oath. He may be a politician, but John has *never* told me not to enforce the law. NEVER."

Will continued to smirk. "If you take care of this, it won't be an issue."

Floyd pushed the wadded paper across his desk and let it roll into the wastebasket. "Get out."

Will stood. "You can be removed."

Leaning back, Floyd smiled. "I didn't want this job in the first place."

"So, you're not going to do anything?"

"Actually, I am." Floyd picked up the phone and started dialing.

"Who are you calling?"

"My first call is going to the Bureau of Criminal Apprehension. The second will be to the Minnesota Board of Animal Health." Floyd put up his finger when the phone was answered. "This is Floyd Swenson, from the Pine County sheriff's office. I'd like to speak to the duty officer about a county official who asked me to cover up tax evasion and other laws he's broken."

The color drained from Stark's face. "This is NOT over."

Covering the phone, Floyd nodded. "It certainly isn't."

A moment later, Pam walked into the office as Floyd ended his call. "Was that Will Stark, the county commissioner? His hair was on fire."

Floyd nodded and retrieved the wadded-up paper from the wastebasket. "He's being blackmailed over running an illegal puppy mill and not paying taxes. He wants us to find the blackmailer."

Pam froze. "Are we going to do that?"

Floyd unfolded the email and nodded as he read it. "We are. I've asked the BCA to investigate the extortion of a county official. Next, we will contact the county attorney to let him know about the BCA involvement and Stark's unpaid taxes and unlicensed kennel. I assume he'll involve the state attorney general's office, the Minnesota

Department of Revenue, and possibly the IRS."

Pam smiled. "How can I help?"

Floyd handed her the crumpled email. "Find out who's blackmailing him and how they found out about Stark's operation."

Heavy footsteps in the hallway preceded the sheriff's arrival. Pam stepped aside so he could enter Floyd's office. "What the hell did you say to Will Stark?"

"I told him I wouldn't keep his unlicensed puppy mill or tax evasion secret while I investigated his blackmailer."

The sheriff froze. "He's running an unlicensed puppy mill?"

"That, and he probably hasn't been paying sales or income taxes on the profits."

Tipping his head back, the sheriff looked at the ceiling. "What have you done since speaking with him?"

"I called the BCA duty officer and asked for their assistance with a case involving extortion of a public official who is operating a puppy mill and has admitted to tax evasion. Then, I showed Pam the blackmailer's email. I was planning to call the Minnesota Board of Animal Health. After that, I was going to give Tom Bakken a heads-up about the case. He'll want to kick it over to a neighboring county based on the conflict of interest."

Exhaling loudly, the sheriff said, "I guess that pretty much kills the leverage the blackmailer had over Will."

Floyd winked at Pam. "I thought that was a good first step in solving Will's blackmail problem. Although that's not the solution Will wanted, it's effective."

"I don't suppose Will's approach was feasible," the sheriff summarized.

"Not once Will had revealed the other crimes he was involved in," Floyd said. "There's no provision in the law to overlook crimes committed by elected officials."

The sheriff looked at Pam and Floyd, then said, "Go ahead with your investigation. I'll contact the other commissioners, so they're not blindsided by the news."

Floyd reached for the phone, "When I talk to Bakken, I'll suggest that he call Stark to discuss his resignation." He paused before dialing and said, "Pam, find the blackmailer. He doesn't know he's lost his leverage."

Looking at the printed email, Pam replied, "'Pay me $20,000 or I'll tell people about your illegal kennel' doesn't give me a lot to go on."

"Can't you tell who sent it?" Floyd asked.

"The sender's email address is a gibberish name on a Hotmail account. Anyone can set one up and there's nothing in the string of nonsense that hints at a name or the originating location."

"It's someone who knows about Will's dog operation, so it's got to be someone local," The sheriff opined.

"Or it's someone who bought a puppy and is pissed off," Pam countered.

Floyd leaned back. "Let's assume it's someone local. Stark lives on a farm near Cloverdale. I saw his mailbox when I patrolled out there. Neither his house nor barn are visible from the road. There's just a gated gravel driveway that disappears when it turns through the trees."

"The blackmailer must've driven down the driveway to buy a dog," the sheriff said. "Will's not the kind of person who socializes much."

Chuckling, Floyd agreed, "He's a little prickly and egotistical. I don't imagine there are a lot of people who drive to his house for parties."

"Who does that leave?" the sheriff asked.

"The UPS driver?" Floyd offered.

Pam immediately shook her head. "No." She punched information into her phone. "Here's his website. He lists which puppies and dogs are for sale and offers to ship them anywhere in the US."

"He ships dogs?" The sheriff asked.

"Apparently," Pam replied, holding out her phone so the sheriff could see the website. "He lists a phone number and PO box as his contacts, so buyers don't even know his physical address."

"Someone's seen his kennel," Floyd replied.

Pam frowned as she thought. Floyd's phone rang, so Pam and the sheriff left his office. "Think outside of the box, Pam. How else would someone get into Stark's place?"

* * *

Pam was studying a Google Earth view of Will Stark's property on her computer when Sandy Maki walked into the bullpen. "What are you up to?" he asked.

"I'm trying to figure out how someone would see Will Stark's dog kennels." She turned her computer screen so Sandy could see the satellite picture. "This shows the house and barn, but I can't really determine that there are kennels there."

"Maybe someone was trick or treating."

Pam gave him a look of disgust. "There's a locked gate on the driveway and he's miles from any of his neighbors."

Sandy sat in Pam's guest chair, then shrugged. "I'm out of ideas."

"Me too," Pam replied.

"What do you know about the house CJ is buying?" Sandy asked.

Pam typed in *Milkweed Lane, Pine City* and waited. Within a few seconds, a satellite view of the neighborhood appeared on her screen. "I think it's this one, the second lot on the right-hand side."

"It's got some acreage," Sandy observed. "Have you seen the inside?"

Pam typed in a search for the realtor's website, then selected the Milkweed Lane address from their listings. "Here are the pictures," she said, leaning away from the computer so Sandy could see the photos as they flashed on the screen during a slideshow.

"That looks really nice, aside from acres of mowing."

"Maybe she's going to let it return to pasture," Pam replied as she clicked on the 360 icon. The bird's eye view of the house appeared, followed by a video of the exterior and buildings.

"It's even got a little barn. That'd be great for storing a mower, ATVs, and snowmobiles." He watched, then asked, "How did they take this video?"

"CJ said the realtor uses a drone to capture overhead video of the properties." The words were barely out of her mouth as she hit the back button on the page.

"What are you doing?" Sandy asked.

"I'm looking for the realtor's other listings."

"Why?"

Ignoring the question, Pam paged through the listings until one caught her eye. She clicked on the picture and then on the 360 icon. They watched a video of a farm including a house, barn, outbuildings and pasture. Then, the drone went higher, capturing a view of the treed acreage and swampy areas included in the property. Seeing something, she froze the image. With her finger, she touched the screen. "That's Will Stark's farm in the background."

"So?" Sandy asked.

"So, Casey Satter took video of Stark's kennels. That bastard knows about the kennels! I also spoke with a reporter from Duluth, who confirmed the drone footage from our I-35 accident was provided to them by him. Raster's neighbor also stated she heard a 'buzzing flying thing.'" Pam walked to Floyd's office, leaving Sandy at her desk. "Floyd, Casey Satter knows about the kennels. He took video of them with his drone when he listed the next-door farm."

Having concentrated on something else, it took Floyd a second to change his focus. "Casey Satter, CJ's realtor, knows about the kennels?"

Pam motioned for Floyd to follow her. "Come look at this."

Floyd hoisted himself from his chair and trotted along behind Pam to the bullpen. He took one look at the screen and said, "I think you've found Stark's blackmailer."

Pam leaned back and smiled. "That's great but how do we prove it? I only have proof from Fallon Harris that he provided the TV station with drone coverage of our accident."

Chapter 12

"What other property listings does Satter's office have?" Floyd asked.

Going back to the realtor's website, Pam paged through the two dozen listings. "There are a couple in Pine City, one in Sandstone, one in Rock Creek, and a farm in Chengwatana Township."

Floyd pointed at the corner of the screen. "Click on this farm."

Pam moved the cursor to the listing Floyd indicated and clicked on the link. The picture was of a house badly in need of paint with weathered buildings behind it.

"Is there an aerial view?" Floyd asked.

"Yes, this little 360 symbol gets us to the drone video. Like I told Sandy, Marvel Erickson, the skunk lady, said she heard one of 'our' buzzing flying machines on the day Donna died." She clicked on the icon. An aerial view of the farm followed, focusing first on the buildings, followed by video of the surrounding overgrown pasture, swamp, pond, and woods.

"Isn't that Raster's farm in the background?"

"I think it is. Let me check the addresses."

"Can you tell when the video was taken?"

"According to the website, the farm was listed last week. There's no time stamp on the video."

"Can you zoom in?"

Pam shook her head. "All I can do is play and pause the video. There's no zoom function on the website."

They continued to watch as the drone circled the property, apparently following the fence lines. "Stop!" Floyd exclaimed. "I see the Bobcat in Raster's barnyard."

The video ended abruptly, returning them to the farm's listing information. Floyd leaned back as Pam reloaded the video. "What are the odds that Satter's drone captured Donna Raster's death?"

"It's got to be one chance in a million," Pam replied as she restarted the drone property tour.

* * *

Riley parked outside the Hinckley fire station between a Jeep and a pickup. The side door was open, so he walked into a meeting area between the fire trucks and racks with gear. Nine firemen were seated, listening to a man discussing respirators. The speaker paused when the rookie walked in. "Can I help you?"

"I heard you were looking for volunteers."

Every face turned toward Riley, and he felt very out of his element. All the men appeared to be farmers and tradesmen, hard-working guys dressed in jeans and t-shirts. After his shift, Riley had changed out of his uniform into khaki pants and a golf shirt.

The speaker, who appeared to be the oldest person at the meeting, smiled. "We're always looking for new firemen, aren't we?"

Most of the men smiled at Riley. A couple smirked. One shook his head like he couldn't believe what he was seeing and hearing. One grabbed an empty chair and slid it toward Riley.

"What's your name, son?"

Riley took the offered seat and nodded at the others. "I'm Riley. Riley Sanders."

The speaker nodded. "I'm Ernie Sternquist. Guys, introduce yourselves."

The men offered their names. A couple shook Riley's hand.

Sternquist waited until everyone was through speaking, then he said, "There's training you have to go through before you're allowed to answer a call. Until then, you should plan to attend our meetings. At the end of the meeting, give me your phone number and I'll add you to the text messaging. We each receive a text message when there's a fire call. You'll get your fire radio after you've been trained."

Gary Proctor, the person who'd shaken his head when Riley showed up, added, "As the rookie, you'll be responsible for washing the fire trucks after every call." The others chuckled, but no one said Gary was pulling his leg.

Riley sat through the meeting, which was actually a training session, an update to the current respirator masks. Following that, there was a discussion about truck maintenance and future meetings.

When the meeting ended, Sternquist motioned for Riley to come forward while the others folded and stored the chairs. "I'm the chief and I run a tight ship. You'll need to stay around after our monthly meetings. I arranged for one of the guys to spend an hour with you explaining the bunker gear, our respirators, and the operation of the equipment. Under no circumstances are you to drive one of the trucks or even take over a nozzle until you've been trained and tested." Ernie waited for Riley to nod his understanding.

Ernie looked Riley over and asked, "Have you ever operated a fire extinguisher?"

"Uh, not really. I know how they work though. You pull the pin and point it toward the fire, then squeeze the handle."

Sternquist unhooked a restraining chain securing a row of red extinguishers and handed one to Riley. "This is an ABC extinguisher. It's okay for use on anything but burning metals. They require a D extinguisher."

"Metal burns?"

Clenching his jaw, Sternquist nodded. "Magnesium has the lowest ignition temperature. It burns white hot and none of these extinguishers or water are going to put it out. Aluminum also burns if you get it hot enough."

"Huh," was Reiley's response.

Sternquist grabbed an empty cardboard box sitting near the exit and gestured for Riley to follow him. Outside, the chief crumpled the packing paper inside the box, then lit it with a match. He waited until it was burning brightly. "Pull the pin, then squeeze the handle. Sweep the cloud back and forth across the fire until it's out."

Sternquist stepped aside.

Confused, Riley asked, "You want me to put out the fire? Now?"

"Ah, yeah. Now, before it burns itself out."

Riley pulled the pin, squeezed and a stream of powder shot out of the nozzle flailing around wildly.

The chief stopped Riley. "You've got to direct the hose at the fire."

Nodding his understanding, Riley held the hose's nozzle as it shot a stream of powder directly at the fire. The edges of the box kept burning.

"Sweep back and forth!" the chief yelled. "Past the edges of the fire, then back again."

Riley shot the cloud of powder as directed and the fire was out just as the fire extinguisher sputtered and ran out. "That's a lot harder than I thought it would be."

Taking the extinguisher from Riley, the chief said, "That's why we practice. A lot of firefighting involves technique and experience."

"Is that what you do during your meetings?"

"We talk about changes to the equipment, repair gear, and do training. If you're okay with that, we meet at seven o'clock on the second Tuesday of each month. Afterwards, most of the guys go over to Smokie's for a beer or two. I'm heading that way now. Why don't you join us? It'll give you a chance to meet the guys in a social setting."

Riley balked, "I'm not much of a beer drinker."

"Drink whatever you want. Bonding with the guys is part of being a fireman. Quite literally, our lives depend on each other. The guys need to know that you'll have their backs in an emergency."

Riley nodded his understanding. "Sure. I'll come along."

* * *

Riley felt even more out of place in Smokie's. He and the fire chief walked in together. Even with that reinforcement, conversations stopped, and heads turned to check him out. Mentally squirming, Riley tried to smile at the gawkers. Sternquist walked to a table of firemen and pushed a chair toward Riley.

The firemen already had an empty beer pitcher on the table and Gary Proctor handed it to Riley. "Get yourself a glass when you refill that."

Trying to be amicable, Riley nodded and carried the pitcher to the bar. A woman, whose gray roots showed through her red hair, looked at Riley. "The same again?"

"I guess."

The bartender filled the pitcher and set it in front of Riley with an empty mug.

"Um, I'd like a tonic and lime...please."

"Gin and tonic?"

"No, just tonic with a lime."

The bartender nodded. "On the wagon?" she asked as she poured tonic into a glass of ice.

"I don't know what that means," Riley replied.

Rolling her eyes, the bartender removed a lime slice from a container and garnished the glass of tonic. "I suppose the cheapskates expect you to pay for this round."

"They didn't say."

"Did they give you money?"

"No, ma'am."

"Fourteen bucks."

Riley paused, trying to remember how much cash he had. "Do you take debit cards?"

The bartender stared at Riley. "You are still in the United States. So, yes, we take debit cards but add a three percent fee."

Riley nodded and handed her a bank debit card. "Add a two-dollar tip."

"Gee, a whole two dollars?" the bartender said without turning away from the credit card machine."

Not catching the sarcasm, Riley said, "Yes."

"Hey, Riley," Proctor shouted. "Can you pick up the pace? We're getting thirsty over here."

Riley set the pitcher on the table and sat down. As he poured, Proctor looked at Riley's glass. "Rhonda forgot to put the umbrella in your drink."

"The umbrella?"

"She usually puts an umbrella in the foo foo girly drinks."

Proctor's comment brought a round of laughter from the table.

Finally catching the humor, Riley replied, "She must've run out."

Proctor took a long pull on his beer and leaned back. "So, Riley, what's your day job?"

Unsure if any of the firemen would remember him from Raster's farm, he said, "I'm with the county."

"Ooh, a civil servant," Proctor replied.

"Take it down a notch, Gary," a middle-aged fireman said. "Excuse Gary, he can't help being a jerk. I'm Oliver." The others reintroduced themselves and told Riley what they did other than being firemen. None of them indicated they remembered him from the death scene.

Gary switched his focus from Riley to the fire chief. "Hey, Ernie, how did your date go with the deputy sheriff?"

Shaking his head, with a grin, the chief replied, "It was coffee, not a date."

"So, she didn't invite you over to her place?"

"She's a nice lady, Gary. Probably not the kind of woman you're accustomed to dating."

"Ooh. She shot you down."

"She's a sergeant, and it was just coffee," Ernie replied. "We talked, drank coffee, and went our separate ways."

"It's probably just as well," Gary said. "She looks kind of like the cougar-type. Maybe she's dating our boy, Riley."

Realizing they were talking about CJ, Riley blushed.

Proctor smiled. "She is! Riley, you dog. I'd never have guessed you were into older women."

Gary turned his attention to a stocky fireman. "Hey, Jimmy, has your wife shaped up her bad attitude since Donna's *accident*?"

Jimmy waved off the question, looking disgusted. Turning to Riley, Proctor explained, "Jimmy's wife has been a little pissy about him drinking after our meetings. I think all the wives will be more...open-minded knowing how Craig adjusted his wife's attitude."

"Someone adjusted his wife's attitude?" Riley asked.

Proctor snorted. "You haven't heard about that? Dumbass Donna walked behind the Bobcat and had a permanent attitude adjustment."

The chief, aware that Riley was a deputy, ended the conversation. "That was an accident, and we all know it."

Proctor took a drink of beer and uttered, "Yeah, right. It was an accident," He made finger air quotes and snorted.

Riley finished his tonic and stood. "I've got an early morning. I'll see you guys at the next meeting."

"Short hitter," Proctor said. Leaning away from the table, he yelled to the bartender. "Rhonda, how about a round of tequila shots for my boys?" He looked at Riley. "You won't pass up a shot with your new pals, will you?"

Riley shook his head. "Not tonight. I've got a big day tomorrow. I'll see you next month."

Sternquist nodded. "We're going to practice car rescues. Oliver is bringing the junker from behind his barn."

Proctor snorted. "Will we be able to tell it from the junker he's driving?"

There was a round of laughter as Riley
left the bar. As he pulled away he thought,
*I'm not sure if they were serious or kidding
about Donna Raster's death.*

Chapter 13

The next morning, Pam motioned for the awkward rookie to have a seat. "So, what did you learn from your night with the fire department, Riley?"

"They were doing equipment training." He squinted at her and shrugged his bony shoulders. The kid really did look like a twelve-year-old.

Pam made a motion with her finger for him to continue with his monologue.

"And, uh, then the chief lit a cardboard box on fire. I put it out with an extinguisher. Cuz that's what firemen do..." His voice trailed off.

"Riley. Did they discuss Craig or Donna, or even their own wives? Remember, this is why we sent you to join the volunteer fire department," Pam explained slowly.

"Ah. Yeah. Well, I think there's a guy named Jimmy, the one who has a clumsy wife. Gary said she's so dumb, she would walk behind a Bobcat and get herself backed over like dumbass Donna did." Riley realized what he had repeated a beat too late.

Pam rewarded his slip with a glare. "Do me a favor. Don't ever refer to the victim as a 'dumbass,' okay?"

Riley's cheeks colored and he immediately became defensive. "You told me to tell you what they said. It's not my fault she was a dumbass."

Pam took a deep, steadying breath and looked at the ceiling. She muttered a prayer for self-control before answering. "Riley, please DO NOT refer to our victim as a DUMBASS."

"Well, what the hell else do you call it? She stood behind Craig in a Bobcat after slamming back a few beers. The guys all said it wasn't his fault. And I think they would know." He stood abruptly.

Floyd walked into the bullpen just as Pam matched Riley's stance, nose-to-nose. "I'm not a dumbass otherwise the sheriff wouldn't have rehired me," Floyd stated, trying to defuse the tension permeating the room with his self-deprecating humor. "Riley, I think they were looking for you in the county attorney's office. There are some complaints that need to be signed." Floyd, ever the emotion barometer, thought it was best to tell a white lie in order to pour water on the heated situation. Riley, ever the energetic dope, stuck his nose in the air and walked out without saying goodbye to Pam.

* * *

At the moment Riley walked out on Pam, CJ was standing outside the credit union in downtown Pine City, waiting for it to open. The manager pushed the door open and asked, "Is there a problem, Sergeant?"

"Not as long as you're willing to give me a mortgage on the house I want to buy," she chuckled.

Elliot Guttman gestured toward the offices located in the back of the lobby. CJ took the realty listing from her pocket and smoothed the paper on the manager's desk. Donning a pair of reading glasses, Guttman perused the information. "We've written mortgages on a couple of homes in this development. It's a nice area and you've apparently already met one of the neighbors." He set the paper on the table and smiled. "Mike Gardner advised me that you have savings and checking accounts with us."

"I moved my accounts here when I relocated from Cloquet."

Guttman took out a legal pad and made notes as he moved between computer screens. "What do you intend to offer?"

"Thirty thousand under the asking price."

Guttman nodded as he entered that number into a spreadsheet. "With principal, interest, taxes, and estimated insurance, your payments will be about two hundred dollars a month more than your current rent. You'll have utilities on top of that." He leaned back. "Are you comfortable with payments that large?"

Smiling, CJ nodded. "My basset might have to give up doggy daycare, but that amount is well within my budget."

"As chairman of the credit union's risk committee, I don't think there will be any problem approving a mortgage of that amount. Of course, I'll have to consult the rest of the committee members, but you've already met half of them."

"I've met half of them?" CJ asked.

"Mike Gardner and I are two of the three people on the risk committee. Mike looked at your credit report and cast his vote before you arrived." Guttman handed CJ a pen and a mortgage application. "I'll ask my assistant to create a mortgage commitment letter while you fill in the blanks on the form."

* * *

Casey Satter and Barb Peterson were having a heated conversation inside the real estate office. The conversation ended when CJ walked in. Both of the realtors seemed surprised to see CJ in uniform. Barb smiled and waved. Casey glared at CJ, then stalked into one of the offices and slammed the door. Still smiling, Barb offered CJ a beverage.

CJ declined and handed the realtor an envelope with the credit union's logo. "Here's my mortgage pre-approval."

"When you said you were a county employee, it didn't occur to me that you were with the sheriff's department." Accepting the envelope, the realtor gestured toward an open office. "Have a seat. I've already drafted an offer for the Milkweed Lane house for the price you mentioned. We just need to add a few more details."

Taking a chair across from the realtor's desk, CJ asked, "Is Casey unhappy about something?"

After closing the door, Peterson sat in her office chair and set the envelope on her desktop. "I *suggested* Casey might have better rapport with his female customers if he didn't immediately ask if their husbands were available."

"He didn't like that suggestion?" CJ said, smirking.

"He pointed out that most women needed their husbands to co-sign the paperwork. He was just trying to move the process ahead more quickly by involving the husbands immediately rather than later."

"Ah. Casey doesn't think single women buy houses?"

Barb opened the envelope and glanced at the pre-approval letter. "Not many single women purchase houses. I pointed out that on the other hand, it was denigrating for him to immediately assume a female customer was married or needed her husband's involvement early in the process."

"Is his attitude going to be a problem when he delivers my offer to the sellers?"

Carefully smoothing the pre-approval document, Peterson formed her reply. "I'll be with him when the offer is presented. His attitude will be irrelevant." Peterson turned to her computer and turned her screen so it was visible to CJ. "I have a couple of documents for you to sign."

After explaining the need for CJ to designate Peterson as her representative in the purchase of the house, the realtor walked CJ through the pages of the purchase offer and the required seller disclosures, from lead paint to the well and septic system.

Chapter 14

CJ was waiting for her lunch bill at Whitney's Country Café when her phone buzzed. After removing it from her pocket she answered, "Sergeant Jensen."

"The sellers accepted your offer," Barb Peterson said.

Unprepared for that announcement, CJ sat up straighter and looked around to see who might be listening. Convinced that no one cared about her call, she asked, "Really? They didn't make a counteroffer?"

Barb chuckled. "It was probably the strangest offer presentation I've ever experienced. Because Casey is the listing agent, he presented the offer. Everything he said or did conveyed his disappointment. The Neilsens kept nodding, then looking at me as he criticized everything from the offered amount to the mortgage commitment and quick closing. He insinuated that you may have overstated your ability to make the mortgage payments, and said accepting your offer would stand in the way of *other interested parties*."

"He has other people looking at the house?"

"Oh, hell no. You're the only person who's shown interest in the house over the past two weeks."

"What an..." CJ cut off the adjective she was going to use when the server arrived with the bill.

"Yeah," Barb replied. "Anyway, the Neilsens listened to his views, then turned to me and asked, 'What do you think?' I told them I thought it was a fair offer considering the location and the time the property has been on the market. I assured them that the credit union thought you were credit worthy, or the manager wouldn't have signed the pre-approval letter."

"And they accepted it?"

"Mr. Neilsen asked Casey for a pen, then asked where he had to sign. We walked out ten minutes later with the signed agreement and signatures on all the disclosures and such." Peterson paused, "CJ, I think you're about to own a home."

A smile spread across CJ's face as she asked, "What do I need to do next?"

"I can drop off the completed purchase agreement at the credit union. Then you wait for them to tell you what documentation they require for their approval. They usually want a couple of years of tax records and a list of your outstanding loans."

"When is my closing date?"

"The contract says on or before the fifteenth. The credit union's mortgage approval will be the determining factor."

CJ put twenty-five dollars on the table, possibly representing the best tip her server would receive that shift. From her squad, she dialed the number on the credit union's business card. "Hi, is Mike Gardner available?"

After a minute on hold, Mike answered the phone. "Sergeant Jensen."

"Considering I'm going to be your neighbor, I think you should call me CJ."

"Your offer was accepted?"

"I suspect you already know the answer to that question. The realtor said approval of my mortgage would determine the closing date. What additional documentation do you require?"

Gardner chuckled. "The risk committee met this morning. We're going to hold the mortgage ourselves, which means there's a lot less paperwork required than if we were selling it to Fannie Mae or on the secondary market. The only thing we need is the purchase agreement, then we can set a date." Gardner paused. "Hang on one second, Barb Peterson just walked into my office."

"Can I call you back?" CJ said before realizing she was already on hold.

A moment later, Gardner said, "Barb just dropped off the signed purchase agreement and other documentation. When can you move?"

Caught completely off guard by the question, CJ hesitated before replying, "When can I move? I have a month-to-month lease that requires two weeks' notice. I suppose I could move whenever I wanted to, although I'd have to pay rent through the end of the month."

"How does next week suit you?"

Stunned, CJ stared out of her windshield. "Next week?"

"We can complete the mortgage paperwork in a day. Once that's ready, it's really up to you when you'd like to sign the mortgage document and disburse the funds to the sellers."

"I guess...um...I need to call a moving company or rent a U-haul."

Gardner chuckled. "You live in an apartment, right? You won't be moving any appliances or a piano. Call a couple of friends who own pickups and offer to buy a case of beer."

Running through the relatively short list of people she'd call friends, CJ replied, "Next week will probably work."

Half dazed, CJ drove northeast on Highway 23 while she tried to wrap her head around the fast-moving events. In Askov, she parked outside the Pine County Historical Museum and dialed her parents' phone number. "Hi Mom. I'm buying a house."

After a short conversation, which included the offer of some cash for moving expenses, CJ dialed Pam. "Hey, Blondie. Would you and Travis be available next week to help me move?"

"What?"

"The owners of the Milkweed Lane house accepted my offer. I just talked to the credit union, and they said my mortgage has been approved. All that's holding me up is giving the landlord my notice and lining up people to move my stuff."

"That was really fast. It might take you longer than you think to pack up all your crap."

"I don't have that much *crap*."

"Your apartment is full of crap and all of it has to be packed into boxes."

Sighing, CJ thought about the prospect of packing everything in her cupboards and closets into boxes. "Yeah, that's going to take a bit of effort." Their conversation was interrupted when a car flew past the museum, going well over the speed limit. "Gotta go."

* * *

On her way home, CJ bought packing tape, a deli chicken dinner and some empty boxes from Chris' Market. *This is insane,* she thought as she drove to doggie daycare.

CJ started packing up her kitchen after dinner. Bailey was intrigued by her owner sitting on the floor while putting pots and pans into a box. The basset flopped down in the dining room and pretended to be uninterested in the activity after her preoccupied owner rebuffed her face-licking attempts.

When the seven boxes from the store were filled, CJ stepped back and realized she'd only packed half of her kitchen. Walking to the linen closet, she looked inside and sagged. Bailey, who had followed her into the hallway, sighed deeply and flopped herself down, mirroring her owner's frustration. "I need a dozen more boxes to finish the kitchen and pack up all the linens. Then, there's my clothes."

In response to her owner's comments, Bailey chirped and wagged her tail.

"Fine, we'll go for a walk."

A block from the apartment building, CJ dialed Eddie's number and sprung the house news on him.

"That's great! Let me know what day you're moving. I'll drive down."

"I'm packing and it's making me depressed. I've got a lot more stuff than I realized."

"If there's anything you haven't used in six months, donate it. That'll save on our backs when we load your boxes."

"That's a thought."

"Stop at the thrift store. They might have a cheap suitcase or two you could donate back to them after the move."

"When did you get so smart?"

"Let me know when you need help and I'll be there. I might even show up with pizza for the moving crew."

"That'd be great." The phone beeped, and CJ checked the screen. "I've got Floyd calling. I'll catch you later."

Floyd's number was being used by his wife, Mary. "I hear congratulations are in order!"

"Thanks. Now, the work begins. I just started packing and I've got a lot more stuff than I realized."

"You haven't lived in the apartment that long. You're not a hoarder like Floyd."

In the background, CJ heard Floyd objecting to the characterization of his accumulation skills.

"Let us know when you need help. Floyd and I won't carry any furniture, but we can show up with a pickup truck and we'll carry boxes."

"Thank you. I'll tell Floyd when I nail down the date."

Bailey, who'd become bored with the conversations, lay down in the grass. Sensing the end of the discussion, she lifted her head.

"Yes, I'm ready to continue the walk."

* * *

Jace McBride glared at his phone as he set up his putt on the green. This was the third annoying text of the day and he was ready to toss his phone into the pond. When he opened the text, all color drained from his face. *I told you, I know WHO you've been doing. Meet me by Devil's Lake at 8 pm. You'll want to see what I see.* There was an attached video snippet that began to play. Jace recognized the pink birthmark on his bare ass in the video. He swallowed the bile that rose in his throat and looked at the time. He had exactly 10 minutes to rush from the golf course to the lake landing just a few miles away.

Jace's golf partner waited impatiently. "Are you texting or golfing?"

Jace slid his club back into the golf bag and picked up his ball. "I've got to run."

"The drinks are going on your tab at the clubhouse!"

"Whatever," Jace replied as he jogged across the next fairway on his way to the parking lot.

Tossing his golf clubs in the back of his shiny new Colorado pickup, courtesy of his generous father-in-law, he began to shake. *Shit! This could all go away. If Dad finds out I've been cheating on his sweet little daughter, this will all disappear! SHIT!* He pounded the steering wheel as he spun along the road to the simple landing on Devil's Lake. It was fast approaching twilight when he arrived and noticed a dark figure in a black hoodie, standing next to a dark Jeep in the weed-filled lot. The license plate had been partially obscured by mud. Jace trembled, shook his fear aside and stepped out of his truck.

"Mr. McBride. So glad you could join me. I really wouldn't want that sweet wife of yours, or her rich daddy, to get a line on these hot "home videos" of you and your piece of ass. No worries, though. If you keep me happy, they won't never see these. Ever," Casey Satter sneered.

"How much?" Jace sputtered.

"How the hell much do you think, Pretty Boy? What's fair? Your meal ticket will vanish in a minute if I share this with your lil' wifey. How the hell do you think Daddy will feel about you cheating on his princess?" The last word was punctuated by Satter spitting out a wad of chew.

"I don't have a lot I can get access to without her knowing. Can I make payments?" Jace shifted his weight from foot to foot while he waited for a response.

"Payments? PAYMENTS?! You're yanking my chain! I want 5k in small bills by next Tuesday, or your rich-bitch princess gets the video! Learn to close your blinds or keep it in your pants, bruh! You wouldn't have this problem if you'd married the hot ass from Tobies, but then you wouldn't have money either," Satter chuckled as he watched his young victim's face go from pale white to red in a matter of seconds. Jace McBride wasn't happy. He restrained himself from reaching across the hood to Satter's neck.

"Where the hell am I supposed to drop the money?" Jace spat.

"Oh, no. There's no drop. You will calmly march your ass to this spot and wait. When I have counted the money, I will give you a copy of the video. Like I said, either learn to keep your zipper up or close your freaking blinds, man!" Casey chortled. His laughter gained momentum and continued as Jace jumped into the driver's seat and threw his truck in reverse. He could still see the oily bastard laughing in his rear-view mirror as he sped away.

* * *

After showering and putting on an oversized t-shirt, CJ walked into the bedroom and pulled back the bedcovers. She checked the alarm clock and was about to turn off the light when Bailey howled.

"What's wrong with you?" CJ asked.

Bailey stared at the bedroom window with her ears on high alert. She howled again. "Knock it off. We live in a second-floor apartment. There's no one outside of the window."

Bailey's laser focus on the window and angry demeanor concerned CJ. Walking to the window, she spread the venetian blinds with her fingers to look outside. She caught a glimpse of something level with the window before it flashed off.

"What the hell was that?" she asked Bailey as she pulled on jeans and a

153

sweatshirt. Grabbing her keys, badge, pistol, and flashlight, she trotted out of her apartment and down the stairs. The parking lot was well lit with no sign of activity. She peeked around the corner of the building, shining her flashlight into the trees outside of her bedroom window.

Am I seeing things? she thought as she walked around the area below her apartment. With no sign of any person, animal, or thing in the branches, CJ shuddered and returned to her apartment.

Chapter 15

Casey Satter seethed as he drove to the remote farm outside of Cloverton. Mumbling to himself, he replayed the discussion he'd just had with Barb Peterson, his broker, in their real estate office.

"Casey, I need a virtual tour of our new listing. Buzz up to Cloverton and make a nice video of the buildings and acreage, then upload it to the office website."

Looking up from the Computer Tech magazine he was reading at his desk, he gave Barb a withering glare. "Why don't you buy your own damn drone and make your own damn tours?"

Barb's smile had been unsettling. Her response was insulting. "Casey, if not for your drone work and the video tours, your value here would...end."

"I put a lot of work into my listings and..."

Barb had cut him off with a wave of her hand. "Your attitude has become a problem. I'm nearing the point where it's more effort to patch up the issues you create than it would be to bring in someone new."

"I have a reputation!"

"And it's not flattering. Have you read your Yelp reviews? Get your butt up to Cloverdale and create a video tour. When you're through with that, we can discuss what's required for your continued occupancy of this office."

"Is that a threat?" Casey yelled at the now empty office door.

Barb's head had peeked around the door frame. "No, Casey. That's not a threat. You're an agent; my employee. Your future is tenuous after the inappropriate phone conversation with Sergeant Jensen and your bad online reviews."

Screw you, Barb Peterson. I'll take my broker's exam and open my own damn office around the corner from you. We'll see who has the connections and earns the commissions then! Satter thought.

Once in Cloverton, Casey pulled into the bar's parking lot. He read the listing's address to his phone and got turn-by-turn directions to the rural property. The landscape had once been pasture, surrounded by brushy swamps and forest. A rusty fire number sign was mounted on a metal post at the end of the driveway with the FOR SALE sign nearly obscured by the weeds around it.

Rather than driving up the overgrown driveway to the house, Casey parked just off the road and set up the drone. He watched the camera view on the controller screen as the drone rose from the grass and flew toward the house and remaining farm buildings. He had the drone circle the house twice, getting video of the doors and windows, then he flew the drone over the roof, which appeared to be in good shape.

The barn's paint was peeling, but the roof appeared to be intact, and the structure seemed sound. The granary and storage shed were in good shape. *If someone mowed the grass and painted the barn, this could be a nice place*, Casey thought as he turned the drone to make a loop around the perimeter of the forty-acre farm.

As the drone completed the loop, Casey turned the camera to show the neighboring property. Spotting a rusty car on blocks behind the barn and a pickup parked next to the house, he decided to fly the drone over the house to see if it was a blighted junkyard, which would impact the salability and value of their listing. A circuit around the house showed no sign of activity, although the motorcycles parked near the steps hinted that there were people inside.

Casey paused the drone outside of each window and door. Through one upstairs window, he watched a scrawny man heat something in a spoon while an emaciated woman tied a tourniquet around her upper arm. Casey watched as they drew up liquid from the spoon and injected themselves. Circling to another upstairs window, he took video of a man moving white bricks and stacks of cash from a suitcase into a backpack.

"Holy hell!" Casey was so focused on the bricks of drugs, he failed to realize the man had stopped moving the drugs and was staring at the drone. It wasn't until the man rushed from the room that Casey realized he needed to get the drone out of there. While urgently flying the drone back towards his location, *I could be trapped in the driveway if I don't leave immediately.*

Throwing the drone controls onto the seat, he jumped into his Jeep and raced away. Once on the road, he looked in the mirror and saw the pickup from next door pulling onto the road behind him. *Oh shit!* Casey thought. Accelerating hard, he tried to distance himself from the pickup, now barely visible in the gravel dust behind him. He turned left on Highway 23 and took off. Briefly considering the bar as a refuge, he rejected that and raced ahead hoping to distance himself from his pursuer.

As the adrenaline rush faded, a thought struck him. *When the drone realizes it's no longer being controlled, it'll go back to the launch point and land itself at the farm! Hopefully, they'll be gone tomorrow so I can retrieve it.*

* * *

Back at the realty office, Casey rushed into his space and closed the door. Leaning back in his chair, he stared at the ceiling and thought. *I'd love to go after those assholes, but there's no way I'm going to drive up to the house and threaten to expose them. They'd kill me. Maybe an anonymous phone call to the cops?*

Casey lifted his desk phone and was prepared to dial 911, then he hesitated. *If I call the sheriff's department, the caller ID will identify me as the person who filmed the drugs. That might open Pandora's box. Shit. Shit. Shit. There's got to be another way.*

A knock on his office door startled him and he returned the phone to its cradle and looked up as Barb Peterson walked in. "Did you get the farm video?"

"Yeah, it's on the memory card in my drone controller."

"In your drone controller? You're not editing it for the website?"

"Can you give me a minute?" Casey asked impatiently. "Something...personal came up, and I need to..."

Barb waved off Casey's reply. "Deal with your personal stuff on your own time. I have someone who is interested in a house with hunting land, and I'd like to offer them a video tour of the farm."

"I'll get to it..."

"Don't *get to it*. Do it now!" Barb left, closing the door behind herself.

"Bitch," Casey uttered to the closed door.

An ad he'd seen while watching a true crime show came to mind. He typed *crime stoppers* into the computer and waited while Google gave him a list of groups who took anonymous tips and paid the tipster after an arrest was made. Picking up the phone, he dialed the number displayed on the computer screen and waited.

"Crime Stoppers, how can I help you?"

"Is it true I can make an anonymous tip and collect a reward if the people are arrested?"

"If you provide us with a tip that results in a felony arrest you are paid one thousand dollars. And yes, you can remain anonymous."

"Great! I have video of a guy packing bricks of drugs and cash into a backpack. In the same video, I have his friends shooting up."

"Okay, I'm going to assign you a report number. The next time you call in, give us that number and it'll link us to your report. Where in Minnesota did this crime occur?"

"I'm in Pine County and it's happening right now! The video was taken at an abandoned farmhouse where the squatters are apparently distributing drugs."

"Can you identify the individuals involved and are they still at that location?"

"I don't know who these people are. But yes, thirty minutes ago, they were still at the house where drugs were being handled."

"Do you have an address where this is occurring?"

"Um, hang on." Casey grabbed his cell phone and pulled up the mapping function he'd used to find the real estate listing. "It's immediately east of this address...."

* * *

Pam Ryan was returning from the restroom when the dispatcher paged her to answer a call. She picked up her phone and said, "This is Investigator Ryan, how can I help you?"

"Hi, Pam. This is Mark O'Connell from the East Central Drug Task Force."

"Hi Mark, what's up?"

"We just received a call from the Crime Stoppers hotline. An anonymous caller reported drugs being handled and packaged at a rural Pine County address. The caller provided the address and video of a person packing white bricks and cash into a backpack. Are you familiar with this address?" He read off the rural address to Pam.

"I know where that is, but we've got nothing on the radar there."

"I'm gathering an entry team. Can you drive by the location in a nondescript vehicle to determine if there's anyone at the location and what the layout is?"

Walking to a Pine County map, Pam put her finger on the approximate address. "It'll take me half an hour to get there. But, yes, I can drive past in my minivan and scope it out for you."

"I'll have people ready to deploy in an hour. Where can they meet to plan the best approach?"

"This address is in the middle of nowhere. The nearest town is Duquette, but the only thing there is a bar and a bunch of cops in the parking lot would stick out like a neon sign." Looking at the map, Pam pictured the nearby town. "The best spot is about fifteen miles west of the address. There's a gas station at Exit 209. We can meet in their parking lot and no one from the Duquette area would have a clue that something was going on."

"Exit 209 is Sturgeon Lake?"

"Right. I'll get a search warrant and meet you in the back of the gas station parking lot."

"We'll see you in an hour."

Pam walked to Floyd's office and closed the door. "I just had a call from the East Central Drug Task Force who got a tip about a drug house outside Duquette. They're gathering an entry team. I'm going to cruise past the house, then meet the team in Sturgeon Lake."

Rising from his desk, Floyd said, "Let's go."

"I've got this. You don't need..."

Taking his bulletproof vest off a hangar behind the door, Floyd replied, "You're not doing this without backup."

"I'm going to drive past the house in my minivan and..."

"And grandpa will be riding alongside you if we meet anyone."

"Grandpa in a uniform and wearing a bulletproof vest."

Floyd walked to his credenza and removed a green Pine City Dragons sweatshirt from a drawer. "Is this better?"

Shaking her head, Pam said, "Now you look like an overstuffed Santa wearing a green sweatshirt."

"Perfect. Let's roll."

Stopping at the dispatcher's cubicle, Pam advised her of their plan and the need to keep the details off the sheriff's radio. "Call my phone if you need to contact me."

The dispatcher nodded.

Pam punched in CJ's phone number as she and Floyd walked to the minivan. "There's going to be a raid on a drug house outside of Duquette in a couple of hours."

"Is this something that's been on your radar?"

"No. There was a Crime Stoppers tip to the drug task force. I'm doing a drive-by to see what's there."

"What's the entry team's plan?"
"We're meeting at the gas station at Exit 209 in an hour to formulate the plan."
"I'll meet you there."

Chapter 16

Pam drove the gravel road, carefully keeping the minivan at forty-five miles an hour. The view from the road was unremarkable except for the posts on either side of the driveway, indicating the chain had been cut and removed. "It's hard to see much of anything behind the overgrown field," Floyd observed.

"I see the cab of a pickup, but there's no human activity at all."

"Turn around up ahead, like you're lost. Then, drive past going a little faster."

Following Floyd's suggestion, Pam drove past the house, going in the opposite direction. "The problem for an entry team will be the upstairs windows. If there's anyone up there, they'll see the vehicles turn into the driveway. Even if the team is racing in, the residents will have five minutes to prepare for them."

"They need to have some people sneak in from the farm with the For Sale sign," Floyd suggested. "Those people can breach the door and be inside as the rest of the team waits in vehicles just out of sight."

Pam chuckled. "I hope they're wearing tick repellent. They'll collect ticks like magnets walking through that tall grass this time of year."

"Collecting ticks so you can surprise the residents is preferable to being shot by a dude who saw you coming from a quarter mile away," Floyd stated.

* * *

Mark O'Connell was leaning against the front fender of a boxy black BearCat SWAT vehicle with four officers dressed in Army-style camouflage, talking with CJ. He nodded to Pam as she approached, then considered Floyd's sweatshirt and smiled. "I never pictured Floyd as a big high school sports fan."

"I'm wearing local camouflage," Floyd replied. "I blend in with all the school kids."

Rolling his eyes, Mark replied, "Sure you do. They all have gray hair and carry a gun."

O'Connell introduced the rest of his team, which included undercover officers from Kanabec, Isanti, Mille Lacs, and Chisago counties.

Spreading a map on the hood, Pam put her finger on a white line northeast of Duquette. "Here is where the house is located. A ten-acre uncut hay field is between the road and the two-story house. If there's anyone in the upstairs rooms, they'll see you driving up the driveway, which will give them plenty of time to warn anyone downstairs."

O'Connell nodded, then asked, "What do you suggest?"

"There's an empty house next door that's for sale. You can drop some of your team there, out of sight from the target house. They'll be able to walk through the woods between the houses without being seen until they're in the yard."

O'Connell turned to his team. "Oates and Miller, you two take the lead. We'll come in as soon as you breach the door."

"I'll come with you," Floyd said.

O'Connell looked at Floyd skeptically. "You're not exactly in camouflage, Floyd. All of my team members wear tactical vests that will stop a rifle bullet."

After pulling off the bright green sweatshirt, Floyd said, "I'll stay back until you breach the door."

O'Connell looked at him skeptically.

"I'm following," Floyd replied, ending the discussion.

O'Connell nodded toward the back of the BearCat. "We've got spare helmets and tactical vests in the back. Put one of each on, then ride with us."

CJ nodded toward her SUV, "Pam can follow behind with me."

Floyd paused before climbing into the back of the BearCat. "You two be careful. Let the task force guys do the entry."

CJ smiled at Pam. "I'm good with that plan. If one of the bikers the tipster mentioned makes a run for it, we'll pull him over."

O'Connell handed Pam a radio. "We're using scrambled radios on a non-police frequency. You can listen in with this walkie-talkie."

* * *

Casey dialed the hotline and gave them the ID number they'd supplied to him. "What's happening with my tip?"

"It's been passed on to the appropriate agency."

"And…"

"I'm sure they're prioritizing it."

"Are they going to raid the place today?"

The Crime Stoppers person paused. "Sir, we can't give you any details. All I can do is assure you that if there's a felony arrest, you're eligible for a one-thousand-dollar reward."

"But those druggies might get away!" To himself he thought, *and I'll lose the reward!*

"Sir, we've passed the information to the appropriate agencies. I'm sure they'll act with urgency."

Slamming down the phone, Casey leaned back and swore to himself. Looking at the edited video tour he'd created for his boss, he weighed his options. He smacked a

168

few keys, loaded his edited tour video on the office's website, and leaned back.

I need to recover the drone. The range is about five miles. If I park in Duquette, I might be able to contact it and fly it from the house to the bar if its battery isn't dead.

A moment later, he was in his Jeep, driving toward Duquette. *I sure as hell hope there's enough life in the battery to fly all the way to the bar.*

His Jeep was the third vehicle in the parking lot. No one seemed to notice it parked off to the side as he activated the drone's controller. A moment later, he saw a picture of grass. *It's receiving my commands!* He quickly reprogrammed the *home* location to the bar's parking lot, then sent a *return to home* command. The video showed the drone rising, with the for sale house in the background. A second later, it rose above the tree line and flew over swamps, woodlots, and ponds.

It took nearly five minutes for the drone to fly from the farm to the parking lot, but Casey smiled when the buzzing drone came into view. It slowed over the bar and lowered itself onto the gravel parking lot before the rotors stopped. The drone's battery indicated it was under 5%.

Casey folded the drone's rotors and was packing it into the case when the drug task force's BearCat and CJ's SUV raced past the bar. Pulling a spare battery out of the case, Casey swapped it into the drone, then redeployed the rotors and set the drone on the ground. A moment later, it was airborne, racing to catch up with the police vehicles.

* * *

CJ followed behind the BearCat as they sped toward the farmhouse. "Do you think the bikers will still be there?"

"There was a pickup there when I drove by earlier," Pam replied. "I guess we'll see if the rest of the gang is still around."

Slowing as the BearCat turned onto the gravel road leading to the farmhouse, CJ let O'Connell's team move farther ahead of them. "I'll hang back and let the dust settle."

The BearCat slowed and eased to the side of the road, stopping next to a For Sale sign alongside an overgrown driveway. Floyd and two of the guys in tactical gear climbed out of the back and walked up the driveway of the vacant farm.

A few minutes later, a voice came over the scrambled radio. "We're through the woodlot and looking at the target from the opposite side of the driveway. There's no visible activity, so we're going to wait here another minute. It'll take us a couple more minutes to cross the lawn and be ready to make entry."

Pam looked at CJ. "It's almost show time. My heart is racing."

"If you weren't pumped up, I'd think there's something wrong with you."

Wiping her sweaty palms on her pants, Pam nodded. "Go time is always a rush."

The radio announced, "No activity. Approaching target."

Pam rolled down the window, hoping to hear some hint about what was about to happen. Instead, she heard the buzz of a drone. "What the hell? There's a drone overhead. That wasn't part of the plan."

Grabbing the handheld radio, CJ announced, "There's a drone above us. That's not yours, is it?"

"Not ours," was the angry reply. "Do you see the operator?"

"Negative."

"Can you see the drone?"

Pam looked out of the window and scanned the sky. She took the radio and announced, "Negative."

"Entry team, be advised there's a drone. We're unsure if it belongs to the suspects."

"Roger that. We're at the door. Roll the BearCat. We're going in on three, two, one."

The BearCat lurched ahead, then raced to the next driveway where it turned and approached the house. CJ stayed back with Pam, searching the sky.

"There it is!" Pam exclaimed. "It's over the house."

CJ pulled ahead and blocked the driveway behind the BearCat. Seeing Floyd outside of the house with a borrowed tactical rifle, she sighed with relief—he'd had the good sense not to rush in with the entry team.

Pam watched the drone hovering over the house. The remaining two task force team members jumped out of the BearCat as a gunshot rang out. They paused at the door, gestured for Floyd to stay outside, then rushed in.

Pam unlatched the shotgun mounted on the divider between the front and rear seats of CJ's squad and stepped out. Taking aim at the drone, she fired once. The drone wobbled, then started a slow spiral toward the ground before recovering and zipping away.

More shots rang out inside the house. The doors over a basement entrance flew open and a burly man brandishing a pistol in one hand and carrying a backpack in the other, climbed out. Floyd, who'd taken position behind the BearCat, couldn't see the man approaching.

Pam swung the shotgun and took aim as she shouted, "Sheriff's department! Drop your weapon!"

The man hesitated, surprised by the police presence outside the house and Pam's command. Seeing only Pam and CJ at the end of the driveway, he ran toward the four parked motorcycles, disappearing behind the BearCat.

Confused by Pam's order and unable to see the biker, Floyd raised the rifle and moved toward the front of the BearCat, trying to view the unfolding scene. He stepped past the BearCat as the biker ran toward him.

From CJ and Pam's perspective, the biker disappeared. A moment later, as Floyd stepped around the BearCat, there was a collision which sent him sprawling on the ground. The biker's momentum was hardly slowed by the impact with Floyd, who was much shorter and smaller. Discounting Floyd as a threat, the biker got to his motorcycle in three strides. He threw the backpack across the seat and switched his pistol to the other hand as he started the bike.

As the biker turned the motorcycle toward them, Pam repeated her order to drop the weapon. He jammed the pistol into his waistband and revved the engine.

CJ focused on Floyd who was initially prostrate. He lifted his head when the motorcycle started but seemed disoriented. Floyd looked in the grass for his firearm when he realized the biker was armed.

Two more shots rang out inside the house, followed by an announcement over the hand-held radio, "Scene secure. All threats neutralized."

The furious biker revved the engine and popped the motorcycle's clutch. The Harley raced toward Pam and CJ. With no imminent threat of gunfire, Pam didn't shoot, taking cover behind the SUV as the motorcycle raced toward them.

CJ stepped into the driver's seat and pulled the door partially closed, providing the biker with a narrow path to the road. When the motorcycle reached her bumper, CJ pushed the door open with both legs.

The motorcycle's impact with the door jarred CJ and pushed her into the passenger's seat. The motorcycle veered into the ditch and tipped over as the engine roared.

Racing toward the rider, Pam pointed the shotgun at the man's torso as he struggled to free his right leg from under the heavy Harley. "Don't touch your gun!"

The biker screamed, "Get the bike off me! It's burning my leg!"

Pam held the shotgun steady, ready to fire if the biker reached for his pistol. "CJ! Are you okay?"

"Yeah, give me a second." Pushing the damaged door open, CJ emerged. She limped away from the SUV and pointed her pistol at the biker.

"This thing is cooking my leg!" The biker yelled. Not waiting for a response, he grabbed the handlebars and pushed the frame with his free leg.

Running footsteps approached as O'Connell moved behind the biker, who'd pulled himself free from the motorcycle. "Is he armed?" O'Connell asked as he aimed his AR-15 at the suspect.

"Pistol in his waistband," Pam replied.

O'Connell nodded, then commanded, "Remove the pistol using two fingers. If you wrap your hand around the butt, you're dead."

"I get it," the biker responded. He carefully displayed his left hand's fingers, then slowly reached to his waist. Watching Pam, who was pointing a shotgun at him, he removed the pistol using his thumb and one finger. He held it out for them to see. "Do you want me to drop it, or hand it to you?"

"Drop it, then move away from it," O'Connell ordered. "Roll onto your stomach and lace your fingers behind your head."

CJ holstered her pistol and handcuffed the biker.

Floyd, looking dazed, approached Pam as she lowered the shotgun. "Did anyone get the license number of the truck that hit me?"

Pam, responding to a buzzing noise, glanced at the sky above the house. "Shit, I think that damn drone filmed this whole thing."

Floyd turned and shielded his eyes as he looked where Pam was pointing. "I suppose we'll look like Keystone Kops on the news."

"When we catch that drone operator, I'm going to arrest him and throw away the key," O'Connell cursed. "Filming a drug tactical team is highly illegal. We work undercover. If our faces are exposed, people could get killed."

* * *

A scrawny man with needle tracks on both arms was led out of the house in handcuffs by the tactical team. Blood streamed from a cut near his hairline and one of the team members held a gauze to his forehead. Behind him came a woman also in cuffs who blinked then squinted as if she hadn't seen the sun in a long time. She too, had needle tracks on her arms.

"We heard a lot of shooting," CJ said to O'Connell as they watched the two people be placed in different unmarked SUVs.

One of the tactical team who overheard CJ's comment snorted. "Druggies aren't known for their marksmanship. The guy fired blindly through the wall when he heard us on the stairs. He was out of ammo before we reached the second floor."

"What happened to his head?" Pam asked.

"I tackled him while he was trying to reload. He banged his head on the bed frame." The guy frowned and asked, "What were the shots outside?"

CJ nodded to Pam. "Annie Oakley here tried to shoot down a drone with a riot gun."

The deputy shook his head. "Riot guns are intended for less than 20 yards. I wouldn't take one bird or drone hunting."

"Yeah," CJ replied. "I'm not sure Blondie would've hit the drone with a trapshooting gun."

"Hey!" Pam protested. "I was a darned good wing shot on pheasants. Dad always said when he wanted meat on the table, he'd take me hunting before he'd take my brothers. Besides, that thing was like fifty yards away. That's a long shot even for a full-choke shotgun, much less a riot gun."

Floyd stepped over and ended the conversation. "Pam, see if you can intercept that video before it makes the news."

"Intercept it, how?"

"I suspect a threatening call to our local real estate office might keep the video off the news and internet."

"But we don't know..."

Floyd smiled. "We don't need to know to issue a general warning to a possible violator."

Acknowledging her understanding that the drone operator was likely Satter, Pam nodded, "I'll make a call and point out the legal consequences of airing that video."

Chapter 17

CJ checked on Pam, Floyd and O'Connell. They were all busy looking at something on Floyd's computer monitor so she walked to her car and selected Eddie's number from her list of contacts.

"What's up?"

"Do you have plans for tonight?"

Chuckling, Eddie replied, "Not other than my usual heating supper in the microwave, then watching something stupid on television. Do you have a better offer?"

"If you bring a stack of cardboard boxes to Pine City, I'd let you help me pack for my move. It all came together today."

"There's nothing going on here this afternoon that can't wait until tomorrow. I'll drive over to the liquor store. They always seem to have piles of boxes."

"Thank you."

"Are you really going to make me pack boxes?"

"This is all happening so fast..."

"I'll walk Bailey while you pack boxes. How's that for a tradeoff?"

"I'm ordering pizza to be delivered in ninety minutes."

"Ninety minutes? I don't have the luxury of activating lights and sirens."

"The longer you talk, the colder the pizza will be when you get here."

* * *

Two hours later, Eddie's knock on the door roused Bailey from her favorite spot on the end of the couch. She stood next to the door, waiting expectantly for CJ to let in their guest. Eddie held up a roll of packing paper when CJ opened the door. "I brought something for you to use while I walk the dog." As they walked to the table, Eddie paused. "Why are you limping?"

After pulling out a chair and sitting down, CJ said, "We had an incident during an arrest."

Eddie popped the tops of two cans of Pepsi and set them on the kitchen table next to the plates CJ had put out. "How bad is it?"

"You should see Floyd."

"What happened to Floyd?" Eddie asked as CJ opened the pizza box.

"He got blindsided by a biker who made a run from the drug house we were raiding. He never saw the guy coming. Pam and I were a hundred feet away and saw the whole thing in slow motion."

"Too bad you didn't take video," Eddie replied as he slid four slices of pizza onto this plate.

"About that. Someone was flying a drone over the scene. There's a video of it somewhere."

"You took a drone video of an arrest?"

CJ shook her head. "It wasn't our drone. We're trying to locate the drone operator. We have suspicions it belongs to my worthless realtor."

Eddie looked at the pile of boxes in the corner. "Is that all you've packed so far?"

"I grabbed a few boxes from the grocery store. That's about all I carried in when I moved here."

"Oh, CJ. You'll be amazed at all the crap you've accumulated. The dog accessories..." Eddie chuckled.

"I didn't think I'd acquired much stuff. But that stack of boxes is filled with kitchen stuff, and I'm only halfway done emptying the cupboards."

"You haven't touched the bathroom, bedroom, or closets?"

CJ shook her head. "Not yet."

"When are you moving?"

"Next week. Although, I have to give two-weeks' notice to the landlord, so I'll have some time to finish up what doesn't get moved initially."

"You'll need that time for cleaning. Besides, you want to move as much as you can while you've got helpers."

"I'd kind of like to sort as I pack. I think a lot of stuff can be donated to charities or thrown away."

Snorting, Eddie replied, "You'll get down to the last day and will be throwing everything into boxes without sorting just so you'll be done before the moving crew arrives."

Looking deflated, CJ replied, "You're depressing me."

Wiping his fingers, Eddie surveyed the piles of folded boxes and tape. "I'm ready to dig into the cupboards."

"We need to leave enough cookware for me to survive the next week."

Going to the pile and selecting the top box, Eddie unfolded it and taped the bottom. "I don't think so. All you need is one microwave-safe bowl, a fork, and a spoon. It's not like you'll be cooking Thanksgiving dinner for twelve." Setting the box on the countertop, he opened an upper cupboard and started loading plates and bowls into it.

"Wait! We need to put cushioning between them."

"They're Corelle. Nothing bad will happen if they rattle around in the back seat of someone's car."

Opening a closet CJ retrieved a bag of newspaper and ads. "Fine. I'll pack the glasses and coffee mugs."

An hour later, they stood back looking at the empty upper cupboards. "That wasn't so bad," Eddie opined. "Let's move to…"

"No."

"No?"

"Come on, Bailey. We're going for a walk," CJ said, removing the leash from a hook by the door.

"But I'm on a roll."

Bailey lifted her head and stared at them. "Come on. Get your butt over here. We're going outside."

"I could pack while you're walking the dog."

CJ gave Eddie a look.

"Oookaaayy, we're walking The Fart Machine."

Tugging on the leash, CJ changed her focus to Bailey. "Get up. We're walking."

As if it was the most difficult thing she'd ever done, Bailey groaned and pushed herself up.

Offering his hand, Eddie said, "Give me the leash. You can lock the door."

Bailey bounded out the door and dragged Eddie toward the stairs. The dog was sniffing the first signpost when CJ caught up with them.

"Being with Bailey is just like being in the Army; you hurry up and wait. We rushed down the stairs and out the door. As soon as we got to the sign, everything stopped."

"So, about the raid today and why I'm limping..." CJ began.

Eddie waited for CJ to say more. "I assume no one died or I would've heard about it."

"There was some shooting, but no one was hit. I threw the door of my SUV open as the biker passed. I braced my feet against the door, hoping to knock him off the motorcycle."

"Were you successful?"

"He drove into the ditch and tipped the bike over. We recovered a backpack full of white powder and cash."

"And the real estate agent's drone?"

"We're about ninety-nine percent sure it's him. He's the person who released the I-35 accident videos to the news you were watching the other night."

"Is that illegal?"

"That's a gray area. Taking video of a police raid is illegal. Selling video of a fatal car accident before the families are notified is tasteless and immoral but not illegal."

"Drones have become ubiquitous."

"What did you say?"

"They're everywhere, like flies."

"Ubiquitous?"

"It was the *New York Times*' word of the day last week."

"Do you remember every new word they publish?"

"Naw, ubiquitous stuck in my mind."

"Tell me another word you've learned from the *New York Times*."

"Ethereal. It means delicate and spiritual."

Bailey squatted next to the post and restarted the walk, pulling Eddie along.

"I had something ethereal outside my apartment window the other night."

"There was something delicate and spiritual outside of your apartment window?"

CJ walked a few steps before saying, "It was more ghostly. Bailey growled at the window. When I peeked through the blinds, I was focused on the street. I caught motion in the trees in my peripheral vision."

"Motion, like a squirrel or bird?"

"I don't know what it was. I just saw motion. By the time I adjusted my focus from the sidewalk to the tree, there was nothing there."

Eddie stopped, pulling the leash to restrain the dog. He looked back toward the apartment building. "The trees outside of your apartment are barely large enough to support a squirrel. What was in the tree?"

"I don't know."

"Are you sure there was something there?"

"Bailey was growling at the window, which is why I looked outside."

Bailey tugged Eddie along with her. "Whatever it was piqued Bailey's interest through closed drapes."

CJ shook her head. "I have venetian blinds. Bailey heard or saw something outside of the window."

"Don't you close your blinds?"

"Of course, I close my blinds." CJ snapped. Reconsidering her angry retort, she said, "There are a couple of bent slats, but they're closed."

"Could someone look inside your bedroom through the bent slats?"

"Not unless they were standing on a ladder. The tree isn't big enough to support a person and the nearest two-story building is blocks away."

Bailey paused at a fire hydrant and Eddie watched in silence. "Maybe it was a drone."

CJ froze. "That dirty sonofabitch! Sure, it was the realtor! I embarrassed him by telling his boss how he'd treated me. He's trying to get even by flying his drone outside of my bedroom window."

"You don't have any proof."

"We might have proof if I get ahold of his video files."

Eddie appeared concerned. "Will he have blackmail material?"

CJ took a second to think back on the evening prior to Bailey reacting to the drone outside the window. "I change in the bathroom. At most, he has a picture of me wearing a long t-shirt."

"So, it's not blackmail material?"

CJ snorted. "No one wants to see a video of me walking around in a t-shirt. They can get that any time I walk the dog after work. But, if we find that video, we'll have evidence that he's been window peeping."

Chapter 18

Oscar Patterson, who had owned the local hardware store for over thirty years, looked up from the box of bolts he was sorting. "Can I help you, Sergeant?"

"Um, I need a few light bulbs. Can you point me in that direction?" CJ motioned with her hand.

"MACKENZIE! Come help the lady cop find some light bulbs!" Oscar barked in the direction of the back room. A skinny, little wisp of a girl appeared, her big round glasses covering most of her tiny face.

"I heard you, Grandpa. Light bulbs." She skittered like a mouse in the direction of the bulbs and motioned with her head for CJ to follow. MacKenzie whispered to CJ as they walked along the cramped aisles filled with shelves of hardware, "I overheard Papa talking about you buying a house from that Satter guy. They said you must not know about all his blackmail shenanigans, otherwise you wouldn't be buying a house from him." She sniffed, then pushed her glasses back up on her nose with the back of her hand. CJ nearly knocked her over when the girl turned and stopped abruptly in front of the light bulbs.

She was trying to process what the teen had just disclosed when the girl repeated irritatedly, "LED or regular?"

"Huh?" CJ shook her head.

"I said, LED or regular?" MacKenzie stared at her like she was deaf.

"Um, LED I guess. What do you mean by blackmail, MacKenzie?"

The teenager gave CJ a funny look and replied, "The Satter guy. Grampa says he's got half the county paying him off. He blackmails people. Like they do on TV. We love watching Perry Mason. There's always somebody who needs to keep a secret. But, on the show, they usually wind up accused of killing the blackmailer." She motioned for CJ to follow her back to the counter to pay for the bulbs. "I would watch out, Sergeant. Mr. Satter might wind up dead. OH! I just remembered something. Did you all find his missing wife yet?" The teen changed conversation directions again so fast, CJ's head was spinning.

"Um, what? Missing wife?"

"Well, uh, yeah. Ashley's been missing for a while now. Everyone thinks she's done run off. Who wouldn't run away being married to a blackmailer," MacKenzie pushed her glasses back up with her finger and disappeared into the back room.

From her car, CJ called Pam. "I just had the strangest conversation with the hardware store clerk. You know, the granddaughter of the owner. She said I should be careful or Satter would wind up dead like the blackmailers on Perry Mason. Oh, and she asked me if we had 'found his wife yet.' What the hell? Do we have a missing person's case on an Ashley Satter? It took me a minute to get the name, but she knew it. How in the hell do we not know this shit? I mean, the hardware store clerk!" CJ's voice amped up. As Pam listened to CJ rant, she quickly turned to her computer and started searching for reports with Ashley Satter's name on them. She hit paydirt immediately.

"Um, there's a domestic that was attached to the DUI charge. Remember when I read the bastard's record to you? Seems he was only convicted of the DUI in that case. There was a physical altercation in the truck. He slammed Ashley's head against the dashboard during a fight while he drove them home from Maverick's Saloon near Beroun. But, get this. She never showed up for court or any meetings with Victim Services or the County Attorney. She just disappeared. And not with any help from us," Pam shook her head in disbelief.

* * *

Later that afternoon, Pam waited until Kerm called *in service* to ask him into the office. His name was listed at the bottom of the report as the arresting deputy. She definitely needed more information.

"Yeah, Ryan, whaddya need?" Kerm was a large, jovial deputy who wasn't afraid to step in and break up a bar fight now and then. He plunked himself down in one of the chairs in front of her desk.

"I have a report here from two years ago when you stopped Casey Satter for DUI and arrested him after he had smashed his wife's head into the dashboard. Now she's missing and he's our lead suspect in a rash of blackmail cases. Can you give me any info besides this?" She handed over his report so he could use it to refresh his memory. Deputies dealt with many drunks on a weekly basis so it wasn't exactly an event that would stand out in his mind.

"Ah, lemme see. Oh, by Maverick's? Yeah. He had been swerving all over the road as he headed west on County Road 14 towards 61. When I pulled him over, I noticed blood running down the lady's face. I mean, she was so covered, her blonde hair looked red. He had split her forehead wide open. I remember he was such a dick. Acted like he couldn't believe I had the guts to pull him over. When I slapped the cuffs on his wrists, it was pretty satisfying. I remember the EMTs were ready to take her in for stitches. Ya know, head wounds bleed so profusely. We couldn't see how deep they were," Kerm took a breath and trailed off. "Why in hell do you want to bring up a DV and DUI anyways?" he questioned.

"Because this asshole is blackmailing several people in Pine County and his battered wife is missing. It's as though no one, including our office, knows where the hell she is. I just hope he didn't dump her in Chengwatana," Pam exhaled.

* * *

CJ called Pam after she parked in Pine City. "Do you have a warrant for Satter yet?"

"On what charge?" Pam asked.

Chuckling CJ replied, "Extortion. Weren't you listening? Even the skinny girl at the hardware store knows he's blackmailing people."

"Last time I checked, 'common knowledge' wasn't sufficient basis for an arrest warrant. Judges like to have more probable cause."

"Did you find out anything more about Ashely Satter?"

"I talked to Kerm, who arrested Satter for DUI and discovered Ashley's head had been bashed against the dashboard. He recalls the EMTs treating Ashley at the scene, but he doesn't know what happened to her after that. She's disappeared off the

190

face of the earth. Her phone hasn't been used, nor have her credit cards."

"That's not good. Do you have enough to justify a search warrant for Satter's house and Jeep? Especially if he took the drone footage during the drug raid. Oh, and I think his drone paid me a late night visit the other night, too."

"Let me gather my notes. I'll talk to the county attorney about a search warrant." Pam paused. "Aren't you supposed to be closing on a house in a few minutes?"

"Oh hell," CJ said as she tried to recall the title company's location. "I've got to go. Text me when you've got the search warrant."

"Do you think it's wise to be sitting in a meeting with..." Pam realized the call had been disconnected before finishing her thought. *To be alone with a man you're about to arrest?*

* * *

After disconnecting her call with Pam, CJ used her phone to find the email from the title company. She realized they were located on the opposite side of the block from the hardware store. Locking her squad, she walked down the block and turned at the first corner. *They're not going to start without you.*

191

The young receptionist looked up when CJ walked into the office. "Sergeant Jensen, I was just going to call to see if you'd forgotten the closing."

"I was just around the corner, so I walked here."

Nodding toward a hallway, the woman stood. "Mr. Satter is waiting for you in the conference room. I'll be down with the papers in a minute. Can I get you a cup of coffee or a bottle of water?"

"I'm fine. Thank you."

Casey Satter sat at a rectangular conference table with five other empty chairs. He pulled back the chair closest to him and grinned. Ignoring his gesture, CJ sat in a chair on the opposite side of the table.

"I thought the sellers would be here," CJ said, looking around to see if they were in an adjacent space.

"They signed everything this morning. Their part was easy compared to the reams of paper you have to sign for the mortgage, state, and county."

"Where's my realtor?"

"I'm representing the firm today." Bitterly, he added, "Don't worry, she'll get the buyer's rep portion of the fees."

CJ slid her phone out of her pocket and set it on the table.

"Are you expecting a call?"

"I'm on duty. You never know when something's going to come up."

"Surely they can get by without you for the next half an hour."

"The law enforcement world is different from real estate. If something serious happens, we drop everything and respond."

The closer arrived with a stack of papers arranged in neat, alternating piles. "The longest one is the mortgage agreement. Once we're through with that, the others will go quickly."

CJ's phone vibrated and she glanced down at the screen which indicated the call was from Pam's personal phone.

"Do you need to take that?" the closer asked.

Putting the phone aside, CJ replied, "It's not urgent. Let's get started."

* * *

Pam located Tom Bakken outside of a courtroom and approached him with the search warrant she'd drafted based on the facts against Satter. She nodded toward an occupied corner near a stairwell.

"We're taking a fifteen-minute recess, make it quick."

Handing him the warrant, Pam explained what they knew about Casey Satter's drone activities and the reported blackmail attempt, including the one involving Will Stark.

"Wow," Bakken said as he read the warrant. "How quickly can you serve this?"

"Floyd and I are ready to go. The BCA is on the way. CJ will be through with her house closing shortly. She can bring in the on-shift deputies."

Shaking his head, Bakken said, "Because the extortion attempt involves a Pine County employee, you need the BCA to lead the search team."

"If you can get that signed during the recess, the BCA will lead the search of the home and Jeep."

Bakken disappeared into the courtroom while Pam punched Floyd's number into her phone. "Tom's taken the Satter search warrant to the judge. He agreed we need the BCA to lead the search so there's no conflict of interest."

"I'll call to check on their ETA. Contact CJ and have her bring in whomever is on duty for the search."

"She's signing closing papers on her house sale. I'll call her in fifteen minutes. She'll probably be done by then."

Floyd's pause made Pam wonder if the call had been disconnected. "Is Satter at the closing?"

"I don't know. He's the listing agent, so he might be there with the sellers."

"Call her now. Warn her that there's a search warrant coming." Floyd paused. "Hell, have her arrest and hold him so he can't dispose of the evidence."

Bakken emerged from the courtroom with the warrant in his hand. He approached Pam and handed her the search warrant. "The judge signed the warrant, and her clerk made a copy. She's concerned about the potential conflict of interest, so I assured her that we would use the BCA."

"Floyd already made the BCA call. CJ is signing the closing documents on her house. Casey Satter may be at the office, so Floyd suggested that I call and have her arrest Satter at the title company's office."

Glancing nervously at the empty hallway, Bakken said, "Does Satter suspect anything? Is CJ in danger?"

Pam gestured toward the courtroom. "Go back to court. I'll text her a warning."

As Bakken walked back to the courtroom, Pam punched a text into her phone. *CALL ME ASAP*. She held her phone awaiting CJ's return call as she walked to the elevator.

Not receiving a response, Pam sent another text. *Call me NOW!!!*

Floyd was standing next to Pam's desk when she walked into the bullpen. "Did CJ arrest Satter?"

"She's not answering my text messages."

"I hate text messages. Call her."

Pam punched CJ's number into her phone. "It's ringing," she said as she listened. "Answer your damn phone!" she said before ending the call. Gesturing helplessness, Pam said, "It rolled over to voicemail."

"Does Satter know we're on to him?"

Shrugging, Pam replied, "I honestly don't know. I don't think we've tipped our hands, but someone may have called him about our interviews."

Clenching his eyes shut, Floyd tipped his head back. "Where is CJ?"

"She said something about a title company, but she didn't mention which company or even which city."

Chapter 19

CJ glanced down at her silenced cell phone for what seemed like the millionth time. The sheriff's office number displayed on her caller ID. A text message appeared from Pam — WHERE THE HELL ARE YOU? ANSWER YOUR DAMN PHONE!

CJ touched *ignore* and returned her attention to the realtor. Casey Satter stared at her for a beat. He was mid-sentence, explaining where her signature was needed on the closing documents. Her phone vibrated again. CJ read the incoming text from Pam impassively. Her eyes locked with Casey's. At that point, she knew he'd guessed the subject of the multiple messages.

"Casey Satter. I need you to turn around and place your hands behind your back." As CJ rose from her chair and gave the command, Casey whirled around and spun like a bucking bronc at a rodeo. He took off like a rocket, shooting straight into the surprised face of the title company's administrative assistant. She gave out a yelp, tossed the papers in her hands to the side and jumped out of CJ's way as she pursued Casey down the office corridor. Just as they reached the double glass doors, CJ grabbed one arm. Her momentum carried Casey back into her and they fell in a heap on the tile floor. He made a gurgling sound as he landed on his nose and broke it. She had just cuffed his hands behind his back when the cavalry, led by Sandy and Pam with Floyd pulling up the rear, entered wearing vests. Pam waved a warrant over her head.

"Casey Satter. You have the right to remain silent. Anything you say can and will be used against you in a court of law. You have the right to an attorney... " CJ huffed and began Mirandizing a still-bleeding Satter.

Pam snorted, "Can you ever not give a dude a bloody nose, Jensen? Seriously!"

CJ, who had righted herself and her prisoner, muttered, "This crap just happens. He ran. You know how much I hate it when they run."

Satter grunted and whined, "Can somebody get me some Kleenex please? This is a brand-new polo and blood is a real pain in the ass to remove!"

Sandy chuckled. "It's okay, bro. We have a nice orange suit for you down at the jail. The gig is up. We've found everything. Oh, and here's the search warrant for your property, home, Jeep and sports car. That's one nice set of wheels," he whistled as Casey protested.

"No! Stay outta my Mustang!"

Sandy, CJ and Pam all exchanged looks as Floyd joined the party. "Looks like Mr. Satter might need a Tide stick to get that blood out. We probably have one at the jail for him."

Floyd, having the best poker face of the three, stared directly at the suspect without breaking eye contact. "Sergeant, take him away."

* * *

Back at the office, Floyd touched Pam's shoulder. Smiling, he said, "The BCA is on their way. The duty officer said their central Minnesota crew was packing up after working a burglary and assault in Carlton County. Now that Mr. Satter is in his new digs, we have time to wait to execute the warrant."

Pam held up a Post-it note. "Do you have his keys, or do I need to find a locksmith?"

Floyd walked toward the jail. "I'll fetch them."

Pam asked CJ, "What's your gut telling you?"

"I think there's going to be a lot more on the table after you watch all of Satter's drone videos."

"After *I* watch the drone videos?"

CJ smiled. "I'm responsible for supervising the road deputies. You're the investigator."

Pam tipped her head back and stared at the ceiling. "Let's see, we're partners in this until there's some boring shit job that involves sitting at a desk for hours staring at a computer screen."

A second later, Pam sat up so quickly she had to grab the chair's arms to keep from pitching forward. CJ's eyes twinkled as together they said, "Riley!"

CJ's cell phone chimed, indicating an incoming message. She read the screen and smiled. "It's a text from the BCA. They're on their way."

They both stood near the exit when Floyd returned with a keyring dangling from his fingers. "What's up?"

Holding up her phone CJ said, "We need to text Satter's home address to the BCA."

Chapter 20

Pam, CJ, Floyd, and Sandy stood on the steps of Satter's house when the Bureau of Criminal Apprehension's Winnebago parked on the street. Jeff Telker got out and crossed the lawn with Sonny Carlson a step behind.

"What's happening?" Jeff asked.

CJ shook Jeff's hand. "We've got a search warrant for a realtor's house, vehicles, office, computer, and bank accounts. He's been recording drone videos. We know of two people he's been blackmailing. We suspect he also recorded the East Central Drug Task Force drug raid."

"Blackmail?" Sonny asked. "That's not something we run across every day."

"I can't remember a case of a drone being used in a crime," Jeff replied. "Do you have keys or are we breaking down the door?"

Floyd produced the keys and handed them to Jeff. "One of the blackmail victims works for the county. We need you to take the lead."

Sonny nodded as Jeff unlocked the door. "Let's pair up and work two rooms at a time.

Jeff can stay with two of you and I'll go with the others."

"Actually," CJ said, "Sonny, I'd like you to accompany me to the garage. I think the drone is in Satter's car. He's been using it to create video tours of the properties he's selling."

A second after unlocking the door, Jeff slammed it shut. "There's a dog."

Everyone stared at him, awaiting more information.

"A big dog. I heard its toenails clicking on the floor. He wasn't barking. In my experience, a dog who doesn't bark is either a really good or really bad sign."

Sonny nodded. "Yah, remember that time we walked into the house with the Doberman? He didn't bark. He just stood there with his ears back waiting for us to move. The owner showed up and led him away. He told us that real guard dogs don't warn you by barking or growling, they just bite."

Barking came from behind the door. Based on the pitch, it was a large dog. Floyd looked at Jeff. "Aren't you going to peek inside?"

Pam nodded toward CJ. "Let the dog whisperer sweet talk the pup."

CJ grimaced. "I'm not the dog whisperer. I can barely keep Bailey from ripping my arm off when we walk. Why in the hell didn't that bastard mention he had a dog when we arrested him this morning? We can add animal neglect to the laundry list of charges!"

Floyd smiled and said, "Give it a try, CJ."

Taking a deep breath, CJ stepped up and twisted the knob. The barking stopped when she opened the door wide enough to peek in.

"What do you see?" Sonny asked.

Pushing the door open, CJ knelt down as a golden retriever rushed out and licked her face. He quickly moved from CJ, jamming his nose into Jeff's crotch.

"I hate when they do that!"

The dog quickly removed his nose from Jeff's pants and pushed at Pam's hand. "Hi boy. You seem lonely."

Taking the dog's collar, CJ said, "Let's see if you've got water and food. Then I'll put you in the backyard while we search your owner's house."

Floyd put his hand on the butt of his pistol and nodded toward a hallway. "Pam, clear the rest of the house while I check the living room and basement."

"I'm going into the garage," CJ called from the kitchen. "Sonny, are you coming?"

"Keep your shirt on. I'll be right there."

CJ was shaking her head when Sonny walked into the kitchen. "What?" He asked.

"Do I need to explain how politically incorrect it is for a man to tell a woman to keep her shirt on?"

"Oh, geez. Are we really going there? It's just a figure of speech." Sonny kept talking as CJ opened the garage door with her hand on the butt of her pistol. "My Finnish grandpa always said that when someone was rushing. 'Keep your shirt on' he'd say. Sometimes he said, 'keep your pants on.' Most times it was to keep your shirt on. He had all kinds of colorful sayings." Sonny stopped when he realized CJ wasn't moving.

"I was kidding, Sonny."

Sonny threw his arms up. "I never know anymore. Ever since that *MeToo* thing I've been paranoid about what I say to people. It's not just women who are upset by things I've said. I was in church last Sunday and I..."

CJ glared at Sonny. "Let's focus on the search, okay?"

"Oh, sure," Sonny said as he pulled on a pair of rubber gloves. "I can search and talk at the same time. Should we start in the passenger compartment or the back?"

"I'd like to first find the drone and any device that could store video and pictures."

"Like a cell phone, iPad, laptop computer, or thumb drive?"

CJ opened the rear passenger door of the Jeep SUV. "Yeah. Any of those, or briefcases and suitcases."

Sonny opened the Jeep's liftgate and stopped talking. "I've got a nylon bag that looks like a case for an expensive camera. I'm going to take a picture before opening it."

With gloved hands, CJ dug into the ashtray, armrests, and searched between the seat and seatback. Finding nothing but receipts and gum wrappers, she moved to the driver's door. After running her hands through the crevices, she sat in the driver's seat and surveyed the space. A charging cord was plugged into a USB port, but the other end was unattached. She found paper napkins, a bag of throat lozenges, and dental floss inside the storage compartment. A metal clip showed on the edge of the visor. Assuming it was a garage door opener, she ignored it, then rethought that decision. Slowly lowering the visor, she spied a thumb drive wedged under the metal clip. "Bingo!"

She heard a zipper behind her and looked in the rearview mirror. Sonny stepped back to look at something hidden behind the seat.

"What did you find?"

"The drone."

We've got you, Satter! CJ thought to herself.

She joined Sonny at the tailgate as he set aside the instructions and lifted the folded drone from the case. "It's not very big," he said, unfolding the rotors and setting the drone on the carpeted back of the SUV. "Here's the control box. It looks like a game console with joysticks."

CJ flipped through the instruction manual. "It can be operated with a remote control or a cell phone that's downloaded an app. The video displays on the cell phone screen as the operator flies the drone."

"We need Satter's cell phone," Sonny said as he folded the rotors and set the drone back into the case."

"I assume the phone is with his personal belongings at the jail." CJ produced the thumb drive she found over the visor. "With any luck, he's downloaded all of his videos on this drive."

"I wonder if there's digital memory capability built into the drone?"

"Is there anything else back here?" CJ asked.

"I haven't opened any of the storage compartments," Sonny replied as he set the drone case on the garage floor. Lifting the cover over the compartment revealed a jack and tools. Sonny set the cover aside and picked up his camera. "This isn't part of the standard equipment," he said as he took a picture of the compartment's contents.

"What did you find?"

After taking several photos, Sonny reached into the hidden compartment and lifted out a prescription bottle. "According to the label, I'm holding 120 oxycontin pills dispensed by an Eden Prairie pharmacy, prescribed for Corrine Markham." Sonny shook the bottle. "I'd say, Corrine has taken about half of her prescription meds."

CJ smiled. "I'll bet you ten bucks Satter's fingerprints are all over that bottle."

Sonny shook his head. "I'm not taking that bet." After reading Corrine's street address from the bottle, Sonny placed it into an evidence bag and said, "Here's her Eden Prairie address."

Entering the information in her phone, CJ said, "That address is Park Manor Senior Living Center."

"Call and ask for the nursing office."

CJ nodded and waited while the phone rang. She asked to speak with a nurse and waited a few moments. "Hi, this is Sergeant Jensen from the Pine County Sheriff's Department. We just found a bottle of oxycontin prescribed for Corrine Markham. The address on the bottle is your facility. Is Ms. Markham missing some pain pills?"

"We control, monitor, and dispense all of the controlled substances used here. We don't usually give out medical information over the phone. However, I don't believe Corrine is receiving any pain meds. Hang on for one minute while I look at her medical records." After a second, the nurse said, "In general, only our terminal cancer patients receive oxycontin, and Corrine is healthy."

"Thank you," CJ said.

Sonny raised his eyebrows. "I should call the Eden Prairie PD and ask them to speak to the pharmacy. With any luck, they'll have a video of someone picking up the prescription for Aunt Corrine."

Smiling, CJ said, "I'll bet that kind nephew probably looks a lot like Satter."

Pam stepped into the garage and said, "We've been through the house. I've got a laptop, bank statements, and tax records. I think we're done here."

Sonny held up the evidence bag containing the pills. "We've got a bottle of oxycontin plus a drone and thumb drive from the Jeep and garage."

Pam smiled. "Gotcha, you slimy bastard."

Sonny clucked his tongue. "You shouldn't cast aspersions on the suspect's parentage. You don't even know if his mother is alive."

Pam laughed. "He's slimy. You're right, whether he's a bastard child is still up for discussion."

* * *

Later that day, Pam and Floyd were in his office when the dispatcher paged her. "There's an Agent Collins from the BCA here to see you."

"Agent Collins," Pam said as she opened the security door between the lobby and their offices. "I'm surprised to see you."

Collins patted the backpack tucked under his arm. "I've been assigned to look at a computer and thumb drive you recovered during a search."

After leading Collins into the bullpen, Pam gestured toward the coffee machine. "Would you like a cup?"

Taking a seat next to Pam's desk and pulling a laptop computer out of the backpack, he replied, "No, thanks."

Pam opened a desk drawer and removed two evidence bags: one containing Satter's laptop computer, the other containing the thumb drive CJ had found over the visor. "I didn't think you were the computer tech guy."

"It doesn't take a lot of tech savvy to boot up a laptop or open files on a thumb drive," Collins said while waiting for his computer to open. He removed the thumb drive from the bag and inserted it into a port on the side of his laptop. "Let's hope it's not encoded or filled with viruses."

"Do you expect accessing the data to be that simple?" Pam asked as the computer continued to boot up."

"We always hope for the simplest solution," he replied. A moment later his computer indicated it was accessing the thumb drive's files. "It's not password protected or encoded. There are dozens of photo and video files." After a few keystrokes, Collins leaned back. "I've copied them all to my hard drive in case something crashes or self-destructs. Which would you like to see first?"

"Are there any labeled Raster murder?"

Collins looked up from the computer to see if Pam was kidding. "Um, none of them have 'murder' in the file name. I don't see any with a file named Raster."

Pam turned and pulled up the realtor's website on her computer. "The realtor has a listing on Dahl Road, in Hinckley. Do any of the file names include Dahl or Hinckley?"

"Yes, here's one named *dahlrd*." Collins clicked on the icon and waited as the .mpg file loaded. A few seconds later, they were watching a video that started with a closeup of grass. The drone apparently lifted off from the lawn, slowly rising as it recorded video of a dilapidated barn.

"That's the barn next door to Raster's farm. This looks like the unedited version that's posted on the realtor's website." Pam clicked on the website video, started the 360 tour, and leaned back.

Collins looked up from his computer, noting the similar buildings in the background. "Pause that until this video catches up with what you're displaying."

Together, they watched Collins' computer until it reached the point where Pam had stopped her computer. "I'll restart the realtor's show."

They watched the same video on the two slightly out-of-sync computers. The website video had been edited, so several minutes of the thumb drive video had been edited out of it. During one of those edited segments, Pam said, "Stop!"

Collins paused his computer. "What did you see?"

"Back up a little bit to where the view pans past the pasture." As directed, Collins moved back in the video to the pasture. "Play this part in slow motion."

Pam held her finger over the screen and pointed to Raster's farm, visible in the background as the drone turned. "That white and orange dot is Raster's Bobcat. Can you zoom in on it?"

As requested, Collins re-centered the image and zoomed in. "It appears to be in a muddy barnyard."

"Remember? We recovered his wife's body in a muddy barnyard behind the house. I think this video shows that area. Continue slowly."

In slow motion, they could see a blurry image of the Bobcat moving around in the barnyard.

"Can you clear that up?" Pam asked.

"Not without using a program to enhance the image. The camera's lens takes a wide-angle view, and the resolution isn't good."

"I thought satellites could see the stitching on a baseball from space."

Collins stared at Pam. "One of those lenses costs a million dollars more than whatever drone took this video."

"Speed up and see if there's a better view of the Bobcat later in the recording."

The drone tour continued, showing most of what Pam had seen on the realtor's website. When it panned back to the pasture a second time, the drone apparently paused, then flew toward Raster's farm.

"I think your drone operator saw something that piqued his interest," Collins said, not looking away from the screen. The drone paused, not far above the Bobcat. Donna Raster gestured emphatically. Craig was hidden inside the Bobcat.

"This must've been taken before Donna was..." Pam didn't finish her thought because Donna jerked back, possibly after being hit. They watched in horror as she staggered, slipped, then fell. The Bobcat turned away from her a second later, then backed up. With her hand over her mouth, Pam gasped.

Leaning closer to the screen, Collins tried to see what was happening. "I think he just ran over her."

"He backed over her," Pam said.

Collins leaned back as they watched Craig Raster climb out of the Bobcat. "He's checking on her. She's still alive." He gasped. "He's getting back into the Bobcat. And he's running over her again."

Speechless, Pam watched in horror as Craig Raster ran over his wife two more times. He stopped, as if to make sure she wasn't moving, then climbed out of the cab and stood over her with his hands on his hips.

"I wish there was audio with this," Pam said.

"I'm pretty sure that's not an option on cheap drones."

"Pause that and give me a couple of minutes," Pam said as she stood.

"Sure," Collins replied. "Would you like me to log onto the laptop while you're gone?"

"Sure," she replied as she walked toward the elevator.

Pam found Alissa in her office. "I've got something you've got to see. Is your boss around?"

Alissa looked away from her computer, appearing annoyed. "I've got to have this to..."

"You and Bakken have to see this. Now."

Pam marched to the county attorney's office where she found him talking to the receptionist while looking at something on his computer. "Have you made a plea deal with Craig Raster's public defender?"

"I made a murder two offer."

"You'll probably want to withdraw that offer. Come with me."

Pam walked away before Bakken responded.

Alissa stood in the hallway looking annoyed. "What the hell, Pam?"

"Come downstairs. I've got something important to show you."

Bakken caught up with them at the elevator. His face was red. "What is going on?"

"The BCA opened the files on Satter's thumb drive."

"And?" Bakken asked.

"You've got to see this to believe it."

They found Floyd leading the BCA agent into a conference room. "We're moving to the video screen," Floyd explained. In the conference room, he connected a cable from a television to Collins' laptop.

"Would someone care to explain what in hell is going on?" Bakken demanded.

"You're not going to believe this," Floyd repeated as the television lit up. A moment later, Collins queued the video to the point where Donna Raster recoiled from the Bobcat and fell. The room was silent until the Bobcat backed up. Alissa gasped and turned away. Pam looked at the county attorney, who was shaking his head.

"It gets worse," Pam said as the video played on.

"That's enough," Bakken said. Turning to Collins he asked, "And you are?"

"Agent Collins, from the BCA."

Bakken nodded. "Send me a copy of that. I have to withdraw a plea deal."

* * *

An hour later, Sawyer Larson appeared in the doorway of the County Attorney's office. Tom met him with a handshake and motioned for him to follow him to the conference room. Larson followed along behind him and took a seat facing the screen on the wall in the large room.

"Sawyer, thanks for joining me," Bakken started as he lowered the room's lights. "I called you in as soon as my office became aware of this new evidence. Evidence from a completely different criminal matter that pertains to your client's case. Instead of making a copy and sending it over as discovery, I felt we should watch this together in order to discuss the plea offer I've withdrawn."

"Uh, sure," Sawyer began to scratch his Adam's apple in response.

The screen slowly played the drone footage BCA Agent Collins and Pam found on Casey Satter's thumb drive. As the video went on and showed Craig Raster backing over Donna, checking on her, then backing over her twice more, Bakken observed the young public defender, certain he was going to have to grab the trash can and offer it to him. Upon viewing the vile footage, Sawyer lunged for the proffered garbage can and promptly lost his lunch.

After a visit to the restroom, Larson reappeared. "I, uh, apologize for tossing my cookies, Mr. Bakken. I can see why you have withdrawn your offer. It appears that you have proof it wasn't just an accident. I do believe I need to have a conference with my client to explain why the offer has been withdrawn. You've extended a great professional courtesy, and I truly appreciate it. Now, if you'll excuse me, I need to meet with my client," Sawyer squared his shoulders, straightened his tie, and marched out of the office towards the jail.

* * *

When Sawyer Larson entered the jail, he asked for his client to be brought to a visitation room while he waited. He was well versed in his responsibility to provide a vigorous defense for his client despite his limited experience. This new video evidence was eating at him, and he knew that it was the proverbial 'nail in the coffin' for his client. When Craig Raster appeared, he blustered and carried on, then stopped mid rant when he noticed his lawyer's lack of reaction and squared shoulders.

"Mr. Raster, we need to talk," Sawyer began. He cleared his throat, lifted his chin and met his client's gaze. "The county attorney and I just met to discuss some, uh, discovery. Now, I know you don't understand what that means. But, in layman's terms, there's a drone video showing that not only did you back the Bobcat over your wife once, you got out, checked to see if she was still moving, then proceeded to back over her twice more." Sawyer choked a bit on his last words, then swallowed and met Raster's glare across the tiny table. "This means that not only was it NOT an accident, the state now has proof beyond a reasonable doubt that you

INTENTIONALLY backed over your wife to cause her death. I have also looked over the report from the medical examiner, which indicates that Donna, uh," he took a deep breath, "had multiple healed fractures of various bones. Mr. Bakken has withdrawn his offer of second degree murder in light of all of this evidence. Now, as your attorney, it is my job to defend you to the best of my ability, however, with the video footage, it will be difficult to prove that it was simply an accident, and therefore, manslaughter."

Sawyer took a breath, leaned back and waited for his client to burst. He was not disappointed. Craig Raster exploded like Old Faithful, swearing, spitting, and pounding on the table. Sawyer remained seated and didn't react to the outburst, except to wipe Raster's spit from his cheek. He had dealt with bullies his entire life and knew if he didn't react, Raster would sit down.

"Now, Mr. Raster, do you understand what I've just explained to you?"

"Yeah, you freaking carrot top! Alls I know is you ain't gonna git me outta here! I told that bastard Satter that I wouldn't pay him for his 'proof' video! You and that Bakken asshole are in cahoots and wanna send me to Stillwater for the rest of my life!" His last words were punctuated with a fist pound to his chest. Larson took a moment and then spoke, "So, Mr. Raster, do you want me to reach out to Mr. Bakken and discuss a straight plea to seconddegree murder? It would mean approximately twenty-five years. Less with good behavior," he resisted the urge to reach up and scratch his Adam's apple.

"Screw all of you bastards!" Raster cussed.

"I will take that as a no, Mr. Raster," Sawyer stood and rapped on the door. The jailer appeared and gave him a look of sympathy as he left.

Chapter 21

Pam sat at her desk viewing more of Satter's drone footage. Many of the videos were unedited real estate tours that matched his real estate sales and listings. Some were half an hour long as the drone flew over farms and neighborhoods around the listed houses.

Floyd walked up behind her as she looked at a video of Pine City High School. Sipping from his mug, he asked, "Why would Satter take a video of the school?"

"I suppose a family considering relocation to the area would like to see the school their children would attend."

Plunking himself down in Pam's guest chair, he asked, "Have you found any others that are suspicious?"

"Not really. Lots of them are unedited videos of virtual house tours. They go on for half an hour or more. He spends a lot of time capturing shots of the neighborhood and things beyond the property. He edits them heavily before posting the tour on their website."

"I suppose that's how he happened to be at Rasters'. He was taking video of the neighboring farm and saw the commotion next door."

Pam leaned back and stretched. "I wonder if he had some inkling there was going to be a confrontation there. It seems unlikely he'd just happen to be flying his drone over Raster's barnyard when Craig ran Donna over with the Bobcat."

"Have you found any videos unrelated to the real estate business?" Floyd asked, switching gears.

"Do you mean besides the Duquette drug bust?" Pam used her computer mouse to select a video she'd seen earlier. "Here's the video of the accident on I-35. It appears Satter got caught up in the traffic behind it and decided to use the drone to look ahead of him."

"Hmm. Have you seen any other opportunistic videos?"

She selected another video from the list and showed Floyd an overhead view of a house fire. "He must've gotten a tip that the Pine City Fire Department had been called out for this house fire. The firemen haven't been at the scene very long. The flames are coming out of the upstairs windows."

"Is there any rhyme or reason to the file names that would draw you to one suspicious video buried among the real estate jobs?"

Turning her head, Pam looked at Floyd. "Gee, that's a great suggestion, Floyd. I'd never have thought to look at the files marked blackmail instead of watching a hundred videos of the drone flying over houses."

The sheriff walked into the bullpen. Spying Pam and Floyd looking at videos, he looked over Pam's shoulder. "What have you found?"

"Floyd suggested that I focus on the files marked 'blackmail' instead of going through the videos one at a time."

"There are files marked 'blackmail?'" the sheriff asked.

"No," Pam replied. "Floyd is just being annoying."

"I'm not being annoying, and I didn't suggest looking at files marked 'blackmail.' I asked if there was anything in the file names that would give her a hint at the content."

Sighing, Pam leaned back. "Trust me, I read all the file names, and I didn't find any that looked suspicious, or would make me look at them ahead of any others. They're mostly a date and a cryptic file name that means nothing to me."

"What did he name the file with the car accident?" Floyd asked.

"It's a date, followed by some letters that don't lead me to anything."

"Is there something special in the naming of the Raster video?" The sheriff asked.

Pam moved her cursor to that video. "It's the date of the murder and the property address next to the Raster farm. That's how he labeled the real estate tours."

"What's the file of the puppy mill labeled?" Floyd asked.

"It's also a date and address," Pam replied, moving her cursor to that file.

"But that address isn't one of Satter's listings, right?" Floyd asked.

"Correct," Pam said. She moved to the real estate website and pulled up their listings. "After viewing a couple of the sold and current listings, I've been skipping those and focusing on the other videos, hoping to find something unrelated to the business."

Straightening up, the sheriff patted Pam on the shoulder. "I think you've got this under control."

"Thank you, sir," Pam replied to the sheriff. Turning to Floyd, she said, "You may leave now and let me get back to my search."

Snorting, the sheriff said, "Floyd, I think we're interfering with Pam's investigation. We've been dismissed."

Floyd stood and took his coffee mug. "I hate it when the kids I've trained become smarter than me. It makes me feel old and unloved."

Looking over her shoulder, Pam replied, "I still love you, Mentor. I'd love you more if you were in your office."

Pam began losing her concentration when viewing another video that was not associated with real estate listings. She stopped the playback and made a cup of coffee. This is boring as hell. I wish I could dump this on Riley. Then, she chastised herself. *Suck it up, Ryan, this is what you signed on for when you wanted to become an investigator.*

Back at her desk, she restarted the video showing farmland along a gravel road. *Why are you making a video of an empty road, Satter?* Pam thought. Farther ahead, a truck was parked off the road near a ravine. As the drone drew nearer, the video zoomed in on two men pushing appliances off the back. Beyond the truck was the ravine where dozens of appliances were piled. The paint kept the metal from rusting, so the age of the appliances was difficult to discern. Still, some of the refrigerators had old-fashioned rounded tops and some items deeper in the pile were avocado green, which Pam remembered from her grandparents' house when she was a child.

The drone continued filming as the men pushed eight more appliances into the ravine. The drone zoomed in on the driver's door as the men climbed down from the truck. The logo read, FRANK'S APPLIANCE RECYCLING.

"Great recycling program, guys," Pam said to herself as she made a note of the phone number from the truck's door. She watched the truck pull away. Once it was gone, the drone moved over the swampy ravine and captured the entire appliance pile, filling most of an acre. The drone continued down the road until it showed the crossroad, which was paved. I know where that is! Pam made a note of the names of the two intersecting roads.

Floyd walked into the bullpen and looked over Pam's shoulder at her computer monitor as she watched drone footage of a lakefront home. A brown plume was spewing into the blue-green lake water. "What's that?" he asked.

"It appears someone is pumping their septic tank into the lake," Pam observed as the drone moved around the property's perimeter.

"Do we know where this was taken?"

"Not yet. Satter usually hovers the drone over a mailbox or fire number before he ends the video. I can locate most of the properties."

"The DNR would be very interested in this," Floyd observed as the drone gained altitude, showing the growing plume of brown in the lake.

"I'm surprised a neighbor didn't call this in. I'm sure they don't want their kids swimming or fishing in this...muck." Pam noted the township fire number posted at the home's driveway. "I'll call the conservation officer to see if this was reported."

"What else have you found?"

"I've got a video of appliances being dumped into a ravine. How many more videos do you want me to view, or can I interview these three to learn about their blackmail?"

"Bring them in. None of them are going to admit anything unless you show them the videos."

"I'll track down that appliance dumper."

"What appliance dumper?" Floyd asked as he went to refill his coffee cup.

"There's a video of a truck from Frank's Appliance Recycling dumping appliances in a ditch. From the size of the pile, I'd say he's been using that spot for a while."

"There's a video of Frank Gustafson dumping appliances?"

"I don't know who the man was, but he was driving a truck with the appliance recycling company name and phone number on the door."

"I have a hard time envisioning Frank making blackmail payments to Casey. He's been in and out of jail a few times. He's way out of Casey's league. He'd squish him like a bug."

Shutting down her computer, Pam noted Gustafson's name and phone number. "Maybe he's the perfect person to testify against Satter—someone who told him to shove it."

Floyd chuckled. "Knowing Frank, I'd say his response would've been more colorful than that. Take someone with you to Frank's place."

Pam paused, weighing Floyd's suggestion. "Do you think I'll need backup to interview him?"

Floyd thought for a moment, then added, "I'll grab my coat and ride with you."

"I'll leave a message for the conservation officer while you get your coat...and your vest."

"Frank isn't going to shoot me."

Pam punched in the conservation officer's phone number. While it rang, she said, "It's department policy, boss."

* * *

The hand-painted Frank's Appliance Recycling sign was mounted on a six-foot chain-link fence just off the gravel road. Inside the fence, a row of rusting appliances and two dilapidated trailer houses with For Sale signs in the windows were visible.

Pam parked in front of a cement-block building next to the truck she'd seen in the video. "Frank runs a low overhead operation," Pam said.

"I don't imagine there's a lot of money in appliance recycling," Floyd observed as they walked through the door.

The office area was as utilitarian as the exterior. A row of appliances lined the office area. Most were relatively new with hand-lettered signs showing prices from $25-100. The shelving on one wall was piled with appliance parts. Most of the part prices were higher than the displayed appliances. An open door behind a counter flickered with a reflection of a television game show.

A burly man Pam recognized from the video, stepped to the door and froze. "I don't suppose you two are here shopping."

"It's been a few years, Frank. How have you been?" Floyd asked.

"You don't give a damn how I am. What in hell do you want?" Frank looked away from Floyd. His lips curled into a smile while he studied Pam. "Well, well. You're a nice change from the usual cops who show up with Floyd. What's your name, honey?"

"I'm Investigator Ryan, the person who came to arrest you for illegally dumping appliances."

Frank's eyes drifted up and down Pam's body. She responded with a glare. "I'm sure I have no idea what you're talking about, sweetheart."

"I've got a videotape showing you pushing appliances from your truck into a ravine. We'll need to impound your truck while we investigate."

Frank stiffened and sneered, "That's not happening."

"There may be a way around that," Floyd suggested. "We'd like to know about your dealings with Casey Satter."

"Never heard of him."

"He's blackmailing you," Pam said. "He took a video of you illegally dumping appliances."

"I think you're mistaken."

"Would you like to see the video?" Pam asked.

Frank's smile returned. "I'd rather show you some of my videos…"

"Frank," Floyd said, "we can overlook the appliance dumping if you were to tell us about Casey's attempted blackmail."

"Littering is a misdemeanor. Put the ticket on the counter on your way out."

"It'll be one ticket for every appliance in the ditch," Pam countered. "The judge might feel that's egregious and slap you with the maximum penalty for each item you dumped."

"I'm not a snitch."

"You're not in jail," Floyd replied. "We're asking you to tell us about someone who appears to be an upstanding citizen."

Frank snorted. "Upstanding citizen. That's a good one. He's more crooked than most of the people in the Stillwater state prison."

"Set us straight," Pam replied.

"Satter waltzed in here spouting off about having a video of me. I listened for about thirty seconds, then I lifted him off his feet with one hand and grabbed his nuts with the other. I told him if he ever whispered my name to a cop, I'd rip his nuts off and feed them to my dog. He seemed to think that was a persuasive argument. That's the last I've seen or heard of him." Gustafson froze. "Did that sonofabitch sic you on me?"

"We acquired his video collection," Pam said.

"I assume he's been busy."

"You might not be the only person he's approached," Floyd said.

"We'd like you to make a formal statement," Pam added.

Gustafson shook his head. "You've got all the statements I'm going to make."

"Do you know of anyone else he's tried to blackmail?" Floyd asked.

"I have no idea what you're talking about," Gustafson replied as he turned and walked through his office door. "Don't let the door hit you in the ass on your way out."

Pam shuddered as she turned the ignition key. "What a creep."

"I bet you're pleased I rode along with you."

Pulling onto the street, Pam nodded. "This was one of those times when I was more than happy to have you ride along."

"Are you saying there are other times when I was less welcome?"

"Don't press your luck," Pam drove a bit, then asked, "Do you think he'd testify against Satter?"

"I learned a long time ago that ex-cons make poor witnesses. Juries have a hard time believing them, even if we can get them into the courtroom."

* * *

Pam needed quiet time to sort through the facts. After passing the information along to the DNR regarding the sewer dumper and reviewing more footage, she thought returning to the Raster crime scene might shake loose something lingering in her subconscious. She was driving to Raster's farm when she saw activity at the skunk farm.

Marvel Erickson waved at Pam as she drove down the driveway. Stinky appeared from behind the barn, apparently curious about the sound of Pam's approach. She ambled across the yard until Pam stepped from her vehicle. Once Stinky recognized Pam, her slow walk turned into an excited waddle. Circling Pam's legs, she rubbed against Pam's pants like a cat.

"Stinky remembers me," Pam said as she slowly approached the homeowner, being careful not to step on the pet skunk.

"She remembers anyone who's ever fed her a treat."

Producing a dog biscuit from her pocket, Pam held it up. "Will she eat a Milk Bone? I keep them in my desk in case Sergeant Jensen shows up with her basset hound."

"You can give it a try."

Pam squatted down and held the biscuit out. "Try this, Stinky." After tentatively sniffing the unfamiliar dog treat, Stinky gently took it from Pam's palm, then

230

wandered away into the long grass. "That wasn't exactly an excited response."

"In general, the skunks prefer moist, meat-based treats. The dog treats are more grain-based. I imagine dogs like the crunch, which is probably like gnawing on a bone." Gesturing toward the house, Marvel suggested that Pam come inside for a cup of coffee.

As Marvel poured, Pam asked, "Have you remembered anything else about the day of Donna Raster's murder?"

The woman hesitated for just a second as she picked up the two steaming mugs. "It was murder, not an accident?"

"The county attorney has seated a grand jury to consider first degree murder charges against Craig Raster."

Erickson set a plate with several homemade cookies and a mug in front of Pam, then she took a chair across the table. "Murder. Huh. I didn't think Craig had it in him to murder anyone."

"Think back to that day. Is there anything unusual that you recall?"

"My days are all similar. Nothing extraordinary comes to mind."

"The drone was flying around, correct?"

Marvel was halfway through a swallow when she choked. Gesturing with her hand to indicate she was okay and just catching her breath. "Yes, there was a strange buzzing sound. I don't recall seeing anything. At the time, I thought it reminded me of swarming bees. I thought the flying buzzing machine belonged to you folks."

"Is there anything else memorable about that day?"

"Not other than the Rasters yelling at each other, then you folks and the fire department showing up. To be honest, that is about the most excitement I've had in several years. But none of that is more than what I told you on the day of the accident, uh, murder."

"Have you been approached by Casey Satter about your skunk operation?"

"Casey, the realtor?"

"Has he contacted you since the day of the murder?"

Marvel seemed perplexed by the question. "No. I'm not interested in selling. Why would a realtor contact me?"

"Do you need a license to raise skunks?"

"I actually need two licenses," Marvel said, rising from her chair. She went to a file cabinet and removed a folder that she brought to the table and handed Pam two sheets of paper. "I need a fur farm license to raise the skunks and a separate license to sell pets."

As Pam read the licenses, Marvel added. "I've got records of all the skunks I've raised, the ones I've sold live, the tagged skins, and the scent glands."

Handing back the licenses, Pam said, "I had no idea there was so much recordkeeping involved."

"The state has their fingers in everything from licensing and vaccination requirements, to health screening and sales tax. Nothing slips through the cracks."

"So, Casey Satter would have no reason to blackmail you?"

Marvel laughed, making Pam think of Santa Claus and his bowl-full-of-jelly belly. Catching her breath, Marvel wiped her eyes. "I probably shouldn't admit this, but the last illegal thing I did was smoke a joint with my boyfriend about 1962. I didn't like it. I didn't get high. And I never tried marijuana again."

"I think we're past the statute of limitations," Pam said as she ate the last bite of her cookie, then wiped her mouth with a paper napkin. "Thanks for the coffee, cookie, and overview of skunk farming requirements."

"I couldn't talk you into staying for supper, could I? I've got fresh liver that I'm planning to sauté with bacon and onions."

Struggling to hide her revulsion at the thought of eating fried liver, Pam stood. "Not tonight. Thanks anyway."

Erickson followed Pam to the door where they found Stinky waiting. The skunk looked up at Pam expectantly.

"I've got another Milk Bone," Pam said, pulling another treat from her pocket and holding it out.

Stinky took the offered treat eagerly.

"It looks like dog treats are a hit," Erickson observed.

"Let's hope it lasts long enough for me to back out without worrying about running over Stinky." As she drove away, Pam cringed at the thought of eating fried liver.

Chapter 22

Randi Anne Murphy had been the Pine County Victim Services Coordinator for over ten years. It was a thankless job sometimes, especially when the people she was trying to help kept running back to their abusers. There were rivers of tears along with late night emergency text messages, begging for help after a victim had returned to their batterer. This was always after multiple empty promises by the perpetrator and copious amounts of alcohol. Randi Anne had learned to keep a new pack of cigarettes and a case of Diet Coke in her Blazer for those late night "victim extractions" that always called for nicotine and a shot of caffeine.

When Randi Anne's phone rang, it was Pam Ryan from downstairs, asking about one of those victims. "Hey, Randi Anne, how are things?"

"Hi Pam. Oh, the usual. It's always raining poor choices in Pine County," she snorted, "What can I do for you?" She crossed her long legs under her desk and leaned back in her chair.

"Do you remember a case in 2023 with an Ashley Satter? Her husband is a realtor.

He bashed her head against the dash in the truck on their way home from Maverick's Saloon. He was arrested for DUI, too," she added.

Randi Anne mentally scrolled through her files. She had always had a photographic memory. It was part of what made her so great at her job and why Tom Bakken adored her.

"Blonde, petite? Had another guy on the side? She never showed up for any meetings with me after I met her in the ER that day. I gave her my number and everything, explaining how important it was for her to meet with us," Randi Anne stated.

Pam let out a breath. "So, she never showed up and that didn't cause any concern with your office?"

"Pam, you very well know that's common with battered women. If they can't get the County Attorney's office to drop the charges, they disappear. Sure, we can subpoena them and do most of the time in felony cases, but I'm sure Tom had his reasons for agreeing to drop the DV charge when she failed to keep any and all contact with our office." Sighing, she leaned forward in her chair.

"Well, the thing is, she's still missing. And I think her disappearance may be part of our extortion case against her husband. It would be nice to interview her. I just can't understand why there wasn't ever a missing persons report filed," Pam took a breath.

"Probably because she's an adult and has no family to speak of here," Randi Anne replied. She had retrieved the physical file, and it lay open on her desk. She began reading out loud to Pam. "When asked if there were any family that we could contact for her in the hospital, the victim replied, 'No. My adoptive father won't give a shit. He didn't want me in the first place. I became a burden to him once my mother died. Why the hell do you think I married the slimy bastard? My boyfriend, Corbin, would come and get me, but that's on the down low. That's part of why Casey smashed my head against the dash. Corbin's besties were all in the bar tonight and got in his face. He doesn't like being made a fool in public and that's what they did.'"

"That's convenient for Satter. But why wouldn't this Corbin dude file a report? Unless he ran away with her?" Pam was brainstorming now.

"Um, let me see if there's anything more in our file," Randi Anne continued.

"Okay, here's something. A memo from my assistant that reads, 'Corbin Baker called to say he refused to testify regarding anything with this case. He was no longer seeing the victim and wanted no part of this crazy dumpster fire'," she sighed. "In other words, unless a female friend was truly afraid for Ashley's safety, there's really no one who would file a missing persons report except for the husband. We both damn well know he sure as hell wouldn't do a fool thing like that and jeopardize his case."

"This makes me sick. I really hate wife-beaters," Pam growled.

"Agreed. They are the worst of the worst. And, after two years, I'm sure Satter has destroyed any and all evidence of possible foul play. There's no way to tell if she left her mascara," Randi Anne finished.

"Left her mascara?" Pam questioned.

"Yeah. Haven't you ever heard that saying? If she left her mascara, she did not 'done run off,'" Randi Anne replied.

"Holy crap. That's so true."

"I heard it on a podcast that everyone in our Victim Services' group listens to. These people are former DV investigators from all over the country. They have some great insight and one-liners."

"Well, if you think of anything more, please let me know. I appreciate your time. Keep fighting the good fight, my friend," Pam wrapped up the conversation.

"You bet. Remember, we work for God. Call if you need anything," Randi Anne replied.

Pam hung up. She leaned back in her chair and looked up at the ceiling. And began counting tiles. Sometimes the job was so frustrating. *Why wouldn't Ashley meet with Randi Anne? Why didn't anyone file a missing persons report?*

When Floyd walked into the bullpen, he was met with a snarl from Pam. "Look at this."

Floyd pulled up a chair as Pam backed up the video. "What are we watching?"

"Just wait a moment," Pam said as she restarted the video and leaned back so Floyd could get closer to her computer monitor.

"It looks like this video was taken at night. I see light coming from between Venetian blinds." Floyd watched silently as the drone eased closer to the blinds, moving toward a narrow gap. "Sonofabitch!"

Pam reached forward and paused the playback. Then she glanced around to see if anyone else was in the bullpen. Seeing no one she said, "CJ needs to fix that gap in her blinds."

Floyd leaned back, shaking his head. "Shut that down before someone else sees it."

"Didn't CJ mention Bailey barking at something outside her window?"

"I suppose Satter was hoping for leverage, hoping to buy CJ's silence in return for not sharing the candid video."

Pam removed the thumb drive from her computer, returned it to the evidence bag, then locked it in her desk drawer. "We need a warrant for the slimy bastard's yard to check for a dead wife."

"Huh?" Floyd asked, surprised by the conversation's change in direction.

"Ashley Satter didn't show up for an appointment with Randi Anne. No one has seen her since the head bashing incident, and no one has filed a missing persons report. I think her slimy husband killed her and...I don't know, maybe buried her in the garden, or ran her through a woodchipper or something."

"Have you done any social media searches?"

"I was just getting to that, Chief Deputy," Pam retorted.

"Good. I will be at Tobies if you need some direction, kiddo," Floyd chuckled.

"Kiddo? Tobies? Is that part of your diet? Mary is just one phone call away," Pam teased.

After Floyd left in search of caramel rolls, Pam began a fast search of Ashley's social media accounts. There was a Facebook page and an Instagram account. Both held little to no clues except that her maiden name was Potter, and she had graduated from East Central High School in 2018. Pam closed that window and opened another. Searching the vital records database, she found a marriage certificate from 2021 in Clark County, Nevada, for a Casey Satter and Ashley Potter. Both were from Minnesota. Casey was seven years older than his bride. Pam switched back to her socials in search of any local girlfriends. It appeared to be very light on friends, which puzzled her. What twenty-four-year-old woman didn't have a group of girlfriends and post about drinking binges and weekend parties? There were a few pictures with Casey and ATV weekends, but nothing stood out as a lead. Typical battered woman, though. The abuser is their whole life, and they're cut off from outside friends and family. A missing person who nobody missed at all.

She went back to the 'About' section on Ashley's Facebook page to glean some information about an employer. She didn't strike out this time and learned that she had worked at the Pine City Realty office after high school, probably where she had met her knight-in-tarnished armor, then as a receptionist for the Pine City Chiropractic office. Pam googled the phone number for that office and dialed.

"Pine City Chiropractic, how may I help you?" The voice that answered was perky and kind.

"Hi, this is Investigator Ryan from the Pine County Sheriff's Department. May I speak with Dr. Johnson about a former employee, please?" Pam hesitated.

"Uh, sure. But, he's with a patient right now. Can I have him call you back when he's finished for the day? Lots of people with bad necks and backs lately. You know how it goes. Once it's time to get in the fields in Spring, all the farmers head in here for adjustments." The receptionist remained upbeat throughout the conversation and Pam's recitation of her phone number.

An hour later, Pam's phone rang. "Investigator Ryan? This is Dr. Johnson from Pine City Chiropractic. My receptionist said you needed to speak with me about a former employee," the deep, friendly voice said.

"Yes. Did you employ an Ashley Satter, Doctor?" Pam asked.

"Uh, yes. Ashley. She worked for us for about a year. Then, called in sick one day and never returned. We sent her last paycheck direct deposit and heard nothing. Did Ashley land on her feet and get away from that husband of hers?" he questioned.

"So were you aware of the altercation between her and her husband, Dr. Johnson?" Pam redirected.

"Well, Cindy, my full-time lady in front, is kind of a mother hen. She told me in confidence that Ashley shared some with her, but that she had actually seen bruises on her arms when she wore short-sleeved scrubs. Whenever I was around her, Ashley seemed positive, wore a hoodie and kept up with her phone and appointment duties. She seemed skittish around me. I don't know if it's because I'm a man, but I wouldn't be surprised. I'm a medical professional, Investigator Ryan. I am trained to notice things. The only reason I didn't report as a mandated reporter was because she was over 18 and he was already in the slammer for the DUI," he exhaled.

"Well, Doctor, it seems you did your best. Would there be any chance I could speak with Cindy? It seems as though Ashley didn't have many friends or family to rely on except for her husband."

"Sure. I can have her call you. I will shoot her a text with your name and number. If there's anything else I can do for you, give me a call. I hope she's safe," he added as the call ended.

CJ waltzed into the bullpen and dropped into her desk chair.

"Please tell me we have something on the missing wife. I really want to nail this sack of monkey shit in the worst way," she moaned.

"I talked to her former employer, the chiropractor in Pine City, who knew she was a battered woman, and I'm waiting for his secretary to return my call to see if I can dig up any more dirt on your esteemed Realtor," Pam smirked. She crossed her legs and leaned back in her chair.

"Is there any family of hers we can interview in the meantime? I would love to ask them why in hell they didn't report her missing when she disappeared two years ago."

"Well, we could find her father, the Potter guy, and go from there," Pam leaned forward to her computer and quickly did a search for Potters in Sandstone. She determined Ashley's father was named

Ralph and lived in a small house out by the FCI.

"Okay, let's roll. He lives by the prison. I say a drop-in would be appropriate in this case." Pam grabbed her jacket from the back of her chair, and the two deputies headed out.

"Let's take my unmarked, okay?" Pam suggested.

"Good idea, Blondie. We don't want to announce our arrival. I'm really interested in meeting a guy whose daughter disappeared two years ago and never reported it," CJ replied.

Thirty minutes later, they crept along the tree-lined street where Ralph Potter lived and parked a few houses down. They slowly walked up the narrow sidewalk to a run down yellow bungalow screaming for a new paint job. They knocked twice and waited.

"Yeah, what the hell do you want? What's that dumb bitch done now?" An older guy with thinning gray hair, watery green eyes, stained clothes and a cigarette dangling from his mouth met their knock.

"Mister Potter? I'm Investigator Ryan with the Sheriff's Department and this is Sergeant Jensen. Would the person to whom you are referring be your daughter, Ashley, by chance?" Pam held the door open with her foot, her first instinct to step back was thwarted by his exclamation.

"What do you mean by 'what has she done now,' Mr. Potter? We are here because your daughter seems to be missing," CJ jumped in.

"She's good for nothing. Done run off with that Satter guy, then split on him. If'n you ask me, he damn well deserved it. Cocky bastard." The ashes from his cigarette landed on the toe of Pam's black duty boot.

"So, what you're saying is you haven't heard from your daughter since 2023, Mr. Potter?"

"Are you deaf, girl? How the hell should I know where she is? She done run off, I said!" Ralph spat the words in Pam's face. CJ had had about enough and stepped in between them.

"Mr. Potter, I need to ask you to take a step back and take a breath. We are only here to help find your daughter," CJ said, raising her chin and meeting his eyes. He stepped back into his house and flicked his cigarette into an empty pot next to the sagging door.

"Can you tell us when you last had contact with Ashley?" Pam decided she would play the role of Good Cop in this case. She knew CJ's body cam was recording this impromptu interview.

"I don't know. She called from the Casino one night, right after her beating, saying she'd lost a pot of money and needed a ride. When I got to Hinckley, the brat had disappeared. You know, she only called me when she needed something. Always having to bail her out until she got high and mighty and married that Satter guy. You know, I think you all should investigate his ass. Lots of money rolling through their joint account and he ain't selling THAT many houses," Potter lit up another cigarette then inhaled deeply. CJ and Pam waited. Silence was usually the best interview technique. He didn't disappoint them.

"He came here, looking for her about a week after their argument, wilder than a wet cat, screaming about her cleaning out their joint account and taking off. I spit in his face and told him Karma was a bitch, then slammed the door. He obviously has enough money to pay for that swanky Jeep and sports car. Ashley drove around the old clunker from high school we'd bought with her mother's life insurance policy. Honestly, I was surprised she even had access to his money. Skinnier than a post and skittish as a newborn colt, that one. But that's what you get for hooking up with a gravy-train who beats you," Ralph Potter shrugged his shoulders.

"So, what have we learned?" CJ asked as they pulled away from Potter's neighborhood.

"Well, I need to find that incident date on Kerm's report and call the Casino to see if they have any available security footage from two years ago. I'm not holding out hope, though. It's probably gone," Pam sighed.

"Drop me at my squad when we get back to the office. I need to pick Bailey up from doggie daycare," CJ switched subjects.

"Why in hell do you need to get the dog?" Pam questioned. She was concerned that she would be roped into dog sitting.

"Well, the Sheriff wants her to walk in the Corn and Clover parade. He can practice walking with her now," CJ chuckled.

"I thought you weren't going to do that."

"If he wants a public relations dog, he's going to get one," CJ giggled.

* * *

Later that day, after CJ had retrieved the basset, she met Pam in the bullpen as she was hanging up from a conversation with the Casino's head of security. She sighed heavily and CJ knew it was another dead end.

"Well, we knew it was a long shot," Pam shook her head.

"Yeah, well, I've been thinking about the tale her *Father of the Year* told us. If Satter killed Ashley, he would be using her father as a witness to appear as though he didn't know her whereabouts. Then again, if she actually emptied out their bank account, the anger wouldn't have been an act. It could've been the motivating factor in her murder. There were 135 domestic murders last year in Minnesota and about 1,300 nationwide. The rotten bastard likely ended her life," CJ finished. Sensing an emotional shift in her owner, Bailey began banging her tail against CJ's leg. "See, even Basset knows how much I detest that dickhead," CJ said as she bent down to pet the dog.

"I just wish Cindy would return my call. I think she could be our best lead at this point," Pam lamented.

"I just don't get how a woman Ashley's age would share so little on socials or have so few friends. It's disturbing," CJ added.

"Maybe Cindy will be able to give us more insight into this girl. Kind of like a mother-figure to her. Dr. Johnson DID call her a mother hen," the ringing phone interrupted Pam's comments. CJ took that as her cue to find the sheriff and off-load her basset on her boss.

"Investigator Ryan."

"Hello, my name is Cindy Wyatt. I was told by Dr. Johnson I needed to speak with you about Ashley?" The voice was tentative, yet friendly.

"Yes," Pam said, grabbing a pen and notebook. "I spoke with your boss earlier regarding Ashley Satter. I have a few questions for you if you have a moment."

"That poor, little lamb. I don't think she had many friends besides that awful husband of hers."

"Can you give me any background on her? Did she tell you anything just before she left town?" Pam prompted.

"Ah, let me see. Well, Dr. Johnson hired her after she quit at the realty office," Cindy paused and then continued. "I'm not sure if there was a huge conflict or why exactly she left. I only know they gave her a nice recommendation and that she really didn't have much in the way of college, but she was friendly and did well with appointments and numbers in billing. We thought she would go to the tech school here in town, to get some sort of a degree. That way, she could probably get away from that husband of hers. I just couldn't ever figure out how he seemed to have so much money, yet she drove around in a battered old car and carried lunch from home every day. She was so thin, too," she took a deep breath.

"She did share with me that her mother died her senior year of high school. I kind of took that as the turning point in her life. I decided to step in and sort of mother her if I could. I have two kids of my own about her age, and I know just because they're 23 and 20, doesn't mean they don't need a mother anymore," Cindy took a breath. "I told her messing with Corbin Baker wasn't a good idea. I mean, they met at Maverick's where they all hung out together. I guess the husband knew him and his friends, but he didn't know that he and Ashley were 'hooking up' as they call it nowadays. It just wasn't smart. I know her husband was suspicious of her anyways. She didn't need to give him any firepower. I guess he beat her one day because he had had a fight with his boss, Barb, over losing a real estate listing," Cindy's voice had risen significantly during her monologue.

"And then what happened?" Pam prompted Cindy to continue as she jotted down notes.

"I got the feeling she wouldn't give up Corbin because she had no friends, and he seemed to be protective of her. I wasn't that impressed by him. He graduated with my son and wasn't the brightest bulb on the tree. I also found it odd that a guy as old as Casey chose to hang around with a bunch of 22- and 23-year-old kids. But, then again, I think it was a bit of hero worship. They either looked up to him or just hung around for the drinks he bought."

"Cindy, do you know if Casey knew about the relationship between Ashley and Corbin?" Pam interjected.

"Well, Ashley didn't seem to think so, but she was just a kid and seemed to underestimate Casey. In that group with all the drinking, there's no way he wouldn't have a suspicion of something going on. Corbin is a good mechanic and works on all their cars, so maybe Casey let it slide until it became really obvious. Like I said, after Casey's DUI, I never saw Ashley again. She called in sick then disappeared..." Cindy trailed off.

"So, Corbin Baker is a mechanic at what shop?" Pam knew who her next witness interview would be.

"Ah. The Chrysler dealership. Next door to the government center," Cindy replied.

"Thank you for all your help, Ms. Wyatt. Please don't share this conversation with anyone," Pam admonished.

"No worries here, Investigator. I just hope that poor kid is safe and in a better place."

CJ returned with her arms crossed and a smug look on her face. "Guess who is basset-sitting?"

"OMG, I wish we could see it in person, but I just got a hot tip about Corbin, who was Ashley Satter's boyfriend. We need to surprise him at work. He conveniently makes a living down the road at the Chrysler dealership," Pam continued. They headed out quickly to Pam's squad and took off.

A few minutes later, CJ and Pam quietly entered the open bay doors to the dealership and asked a navy-blue clad mechanic to point them in the direction of Corbin Baker. All eyes turned as the two female deputies approached a blonde-haired kid, who had a Jeep up on a lift.

"Corbin Baker?" Pam questioned.

"Yeah. What do you need?" he answered, wiping his hands on a blue rag.

"We'd like to talk to you about Ashley Satter," the two women gauged his reaction as Pam spoke her name. The mechanic one auto bay over, seemed to perk up at the question. He was a tall, heavy-built kid, with greasy black hair that flopped down over his safety goggles. CJ caught the lift of his head and decided to keep an eye on him while Pam continued to question Corbin.

"I, uh, don't know much. She just up and ran off two years ago. We were friends. That's it. I felt sorry for her," he held his palms face up.

"It's come to our attention you were probably the last person to see her. There hasn't been any indication she took off and started a new life according to our sources," Pam embellished.

"Hey now, I called the Victim's Office and told them I didn't want any part of that court thing against her husband. She texted me once after that night, begging me to come get her from the Casino. Said she needed a ride cuz her old car broke down. I didn't see the text right away because I had been drinking a bit and passed out on the couch, but Carter here," he motioned towards the nervous oily guy next to him, "was with me at my house when she texted me." CJ was now openly staring at the guy whose name was Carter. She knew by his body language. He was getting ready to run and he didn't disappoint. The moment Corbin linked him to the last text sent from the missing woman, he bolted.

"SHIT!" CJ grabbed her mic and called for all available units in the area to head to their location. Carter had a head start and jumped into a ratty old car parked in the front row of the dealership. His tires spun as CJ jumped into her squad car.

"618, Pine County. In pursuit of a suspect headed toward County Road 11," CJ yelled, alerting all officers on that channel of their pursuit and providing a vehicle description.

Pam was right behind her and barely got the passenger door shut as CJ took off, lights and sirens blaring.

"Okay, so obviously, this guy knows something. He's a material witness in the disappearance of Ashley Satter," Pam stated as CJ gunned the engine and took a hard right onto County Road 11.

Sandy Maki, who was eastbound on County Road 11 heading back into town, heard the call over the radio. Seconds later, he watched as a crappy tan jalopy passed him doing 90 in the other direction. He slammed on his brakes, did a three-point turn, and accelerated after the beater, activating his lights and siren. "614-Pine County. I am in pursuit," he informed dispatch.

As CJ drove, Pam called Sandy on his cell, giving him an update.

"He is a material witness in Satter's wife's disappearance. He may elevate himself to suspect after this little charade,"

Pam informed him. They disconnected and continued on towards Pokegama Lake. Sandy continued to pursue the tiny rust bucket and as they neared the public access to Pokegama Lake, the fleeing car swerved and took a hard right. He knew the car wasn't going to make the turn where a huge oak tree flanked the entrance to the landing. Sandy began tapping his brakes to slow himself down. He watched in disbelief as the driver seemingly steered his car right smack into the trunk of the old oak tree.

Sandy was out the driver's door of his squad shortly after the tan car's heavy impact. The sound of glass and metal hitting wood and shattering met his ears as he weaved out of the way of the flying debris. He was thinking *this was a non-survivable crash* yet hoped for the best.

As he approached the wreck, he could see slight movement from the driver. The man's head was against the deflated airbag, a large gash running the full length of his forehead. He was murmuring something as Sandy approached him.

"Sir, hang on. An ambulance is on its way," he keyed up his mic and asked dispatch to send an ambulance to his location.

"I didn't mean to. I had to. I mean, I needed the money to pay Satter off. She had the money. Corbin was passed out...I just read the text...." the driver was babbling softly now and slowly losing consciousness.

Sandy struggled to hear what he was saying while applying pressure to the gash on his forehead. "I didn't mean to...she fought so hard...the well was right there...the Amish don't cover their wells...told her we were going to Maverick's...meet Corbin..." his voice trailed off as he struggled to breathe. Sandy knew the ambulance would probably not make it in time to save this guy.

Pam and CJ raced to the driver's door as Carter Miller took his last breath. Pam edged beside Sandy. "Aw shit. Was he conscious when you got to him? Did he say anything?"

"He was mumbling stuff. It didn't make any sense to me."

* * *

Later in the bullpen, Pam, CJ, Sandy and Floyd sat around debriefing from the fatal wreck that seemed to solve one mystery. "He said he was at Corbin's house when Ashley texted him, telling him to pick her up. He referred to having to pay Satter off and knew that Ashley had the money he needed. Seems as though he went in Corbin's place to pick her up at the Casino, there was an altercation, she fought him hard, and he ended up dumping her in one of the wells owned by the Amish," Sandy relayed.

"Well, it makes sense now why he ran when we started questioning Corbin. Pretty soon, he would have put two and two together and figured out that Carter had read his phone while he was passed out drunk on the couch. Ashley would willingly go with him if she knew him from hanging out as a group at Maverick's," Pam took a breath.

"Yeah. Carter mentioned Maverick's. Guess he told her that's where they were going to meet Corbin in order to get her to leave the Casino with him," Sandy added.

"Well, I really liked my bastard realtor for his wife's demise, but I wonder what the hell he had on Carter?" CJ stated.

"And now, not only do we need to search through Satter's blackmail files for that information, we also need to search a few wells off of Hinckley Road," Pam jumped in.

"Madam Investigator, you need to get some search warrants," Floyd suggested.

"Yeah. I imagine we should call the BCA once we find her. Too bad we don't know exactly where she is. I better call in the Minnesota Search and Rescue Dog Association. We will have better luck with a cadaver dog. That poor kid," Pam's voice trailed off.

The group sat for a moment in silence. Even though the officers appeared to be hardened to the atrocities that society threw at them, their hearts were still human. They had entered this profession to serve and protect. They were unable to save Ashley, but still had to serve her by finding her remains and giving her the final resting place she deserved.

Chapter 23

Pam and CJ were studying a map on the hood of CJ's SUV when a black Chevrolet Suburban parked next to them with a logo on the door. The Minnesota Search and Rescue Dog Association team had arrived. Following them was a BCA mobile crime lab.

The young man and woman who emerged from the SARDA Suburban were trim and fit, appearing capable of running a marathon. CJ turned to Pam and whispered, "Please tell me we won't have to run along behind the dogs as they search."

Pam smiled and replied, "You should be in condition. You run behind your basset a couple of times a day."

"Get serious," CJ replied. "Bailey spends more time sniffing than running. I suspect the SARDA dogs are more...focused."

Pam shook hands with the male dog handler, "I'm Pam Ryan, the Pine County Sheriff's Department investigator. This is Sergeant Jensen."

"I'm Tyler Longbaugh. This is my partner, Alice Engh."

The BCA techs joined the group and introduced themselves. "I'm Jeff Telker. This is Sonny Carlson."

Pam smiled and shook Sonny's hand. "I don't think we require an update on your genealogy today."

With a staged look of injury, Sonny said, "My genealogy? Have I ever bored you with stories about my long dead Swedish and Finnish relatives?"

Changing the subject, Jeff nodded toward the map spread on the hood of Pam's SUV. "What's the plan?"

The group followed Pam and gathered around the map. "We received a tip that a missing woman was killed, and her body dumped near Hinckley."

"How reliable is your source?" Jeff asked.

"The information came in a deathbed confession from the murderer. He admitted to the homicide and indicated the general area where he'd disposed of the body." Pam paused and circled the rural area around Hinckley with her finger. "He didn't give us an address or specific location, but we know he disposed of the body somewhere between leaving the casino and arriving in Beroun."

Pointing out areas highlighted in yellow, CJ added, "The highlighted properties are abandoned or unoccupied buildings. We think the murderer was looking for a place where he could dispose of the body quickly, and we believe his local knowledge would've led him to an abandoned house, unused septic system, or old well as a quick disposal site."

Sonny leaned over the map and pointed at several areas with tiny cattail logos. "Don't you think he'd use one of these swampy areas as a dump site?"

Pam cocked her head. "We feel the swamps are a second priority to these abandoned farms. Someone might've noticed the decomposition smell if the body had been left along a road or near an occupied residence. There have also been several hunting seasons since the murder and a lot of the wooded and swampy areas have been crisscrossed by hunters."

Alice studied the map, then looked at her partner. "If we split into two teams, the dogs should be able to check out all highlighted properties in a couple of hours. If we don't get a hit, we can gather back here at noon and develop an afternoon strategy."

"Watch out for buggies," Pam advised.

"Buggies?" Alice asked.

"There are Amish farmers in the area. They ride up and down the roads in their horse-drawn buggies and wagons."

CJ nodded. "Many of the properties we've highlighted are abandoned farms, or Amish farms with abandoned wells."

They agreed to have Pam's team start closest to the casino. Jeff and Pam moved the SARDA canine kennel into the rear of Pam's SUV while the dog sat obediently at Alice's side. CJ and Sonny rode with Tyler and Prince in the SARDA Suburban to search the properties nearer Beroun, on the southern end of the murderer's route.

"Tell me how Bingo works," Pam said as they drove toward the casino.

"I bring him to the area we're going to search, then I let him off the leash. He casts around the area, sniffing for the distinctive decomposition chemicals a decaying corpse emits. If he scents a cadaver, he'll sit down and look at me."

From the back seat, Jeff added, "That's where Sonny and I step in. We'll establish a secure perimeter and collect evidence as we uncover the body."

"The killer didn't have much time between his two documented stops, so we know he didn't drive far from Hinckley Road and didn't have to work very long to uncover the spot where he dumped the body. He claimed it was in a well."

Alice looked at the map, which had been folded open to show the area around a horse arena. "Is there one spot you're more suspicious about than the others?"

"There are two that jumped out at me," Pam replied. "One is an unoccupied house. The Amish grandparents were living next to their son's family. They moved into his house when they caught Covid, and their house had been empty for several years. That's on an unmarked township road between the casino and the horse arena. The other is a remote barn, set back from the owner's house. It has an old broken windmill over a well. The windmill is visible from Hinckley Road."

"Are there any likely spots for CJ's team?" Jeff asked.

"The first place they're going to check is a lot where a house burned down a couple of years ago. It's never been rebuilt, and the acreage is for sale. They also have a couple of run-down hunting shacks closer to Chengwatana State Forest."

Unfolding another section of the map, Alice asked, "What are the rest of the properties you've highlighted?"

"They're places that were built in the days of hand-dug wells. Some are barns and a couple of them are houses. I think the houses are unlikely because they're occupied. The others are farther from Hinckley Road than I think the killer would've traveled. If we come up empty on the likely spots, we move down the list."

"This looks like something out of a horror movie," Alice said as Pam parked in the driveway of the unoccupied Amish house. "I can almost see Freddy Krueger running out of the front door."

Pam glared at Alice. "You *could* keep those thoughts to yourself."

Alice chuckled as she stepped from the SUV. As she clipped the leash to Bingo's vest, she smiled. "Tyler often accuses me of oversharing my thoughts."

The trio walked the driveway toward the house and hesitated at a broken gate in the wooden fence. "I think the hand pump is behind the house. We should poke around the foundation too. There's probably a crawl space under the structure and an outhouse near the woods."

When Alice stopped walking, Bingo sat while she unclipped his leash. Gesturing toward the house, she ordered, "Search!"

Bingo raced ahead and stopped at the corner of a trellis to lift his leg. Jeff chuckled and said, "I guess a guy has his priorities."

After relieving himself, Bingo trotted around the perimeter of the wooden fence with his nose high in the air. Completing the loop, he zig-zagged across the yard. He paused at the corner of the house, turning his head as if unsure of which way to turn.

"He hasn't gone near the pump or outhouse," Pam whispered.

Alice nodded. "Let him do his thing. He'll get to them."

Bingo turned his head from side to side, sniffing the mild breeze from a nearby group of apple trees. Pam chuckled, "He acts like CJ's basset hound when she smells a bunny."

Bingo took a tentative step toward the well, sniffed the air again, then made a bee-line for the old hand pump. After one sniff at the base of the pump, he dropped to his belly and turned toward Alice, whimpering.

Alice looked at Pam and raised her eyebrows. "I think my job is done and yours is just beginning."

As they walked toward the dog, Pam asked, "What do you do with Bingo now?"

Ignoring the question, Alice bent down to ruffle Bingo's ears and praise him. She removed a toy rope from her pocket and gave it to Bingo as she reattached his leash. "Heel," she ordered before leading him toward the SUV. Over her shoulder she said, "Good luck."

Jeff pulled on a pair of purple gloves, then knelt next to the wooden well cover. "It looks like someone ripped this loose a while ago." With a tug, he pulled the cover aside, then shone a flashlight into the well.

"What do you see?" Pam asked as she donned gloves.

"Water and an athletic shoe."

"Shit."

Jeff stood and brushed the dirt off his hands and knees. "Yeah, it's heaven and hell all in the same discovery. We accomplished what we set out to do and found what no one wants to see."

Pam punched CJ's cell phone number into her phone and waited a couple of rings before she answered. "We've found remains. I'll call the M.E. and wait here for you," she quickly relayed the location and disconnected.

Jeff was also on his cell phone, speaking to Sonny. "Bring the Winnebago." He looked at the well and added, "We're going to need a hoist, SCUBA gear, and help with the recovery."

After they ended their calls, Pam stared at the open hole. "What's she going to look like after several years in a well?"

"I think you know the answer," Jeff replied. After a beat, he added, "Alice said something about a horror movie when we arrived..."

"Yeah," Pam replied. She walked away and punched Floyd's number into her phone. When he answered she said, "We found her. Tell the sheriff."

"Where?"

"In a well. An abandoned house between Hinckley and Beroun."

"I assume you're going to notify her father."

"I was planning to wait until we have a positive ID." Pinching the bridge of her nose, she corrected herself. "We need the name of her dentist."

"The sheriff will want to announce the discovery of human remains and to thank the SARDA folks. People will connect the dots to who's missing. There will be speculation on the internet, if not the news. I'll drive up after I tell the sheriff. Where exactly are you?"

"There's no fire number. We're less than a quarter mile from the arena at one of the Amish houses."

"I'll look for the flashing red and blue lights."

The trip from the recovery scene to Ralph Potter's rundown Sandstone house took Pam twenty minutes. She approached the front door, then steeled herself for the thankless task of informing Potter of the likely discovery of his daughter's body. After ringing the doorbell, she listened to the muffled voices on a television somewhere inside the house.

Potter's appearance was as unfortunate as the decrepit house. A wave of cigarette smoke swirled out of the door as he glared at Pam. "What?"

"May I come in?"

Potter took a drag from his cigarette, then exhaled the smoke into Pam's face. "You got a warrant?"

"I've got news about Ashley."

Wrinkling his nose, Potter gave Pam a sour look. "Didn't I make it clear the last time you were here? I don't give a shit about her."

Pam lost interest in being polite and blurted out, "We have located female remains that may belong to Ashley."

Potter blinked but seemed unmoved.

"Do you have anything that might have her DNA? Maybe a toothbrush, hairbrush, or makeup?"

"She took all her stuff when she moved out to marry that realtor. What she left behind, I threw out."

"Who was her dentist?"

"Dentist? I couldn't afford to take her to a dentist after her mom died."

"Could I look in her bedroom?"

Potter took another drag on his cigarette. Anticipating another cloud of smoke in her face, Pam stepped back. Instead, Potter blew the smoke aside. He pushed the screen door open, dropped his cigarette on the top step, then crushed it with the toe of his shoe. Nodding his head, he indicated Pam should enter. "If you gotta look, look. There ain't nothing there."

The house's entryway was filthy, with mud ground into the linoleum floor. Two threadbare jackets hung from pegs next to a broken off peg. Feeling uneasy about the situation and the house, Pam pulled a pair of latex gloves from her pocket.

"You make it look like you're collecting evidence."

"I don't want my DNA to contaminate anything of Ashley's," she replied. In actuality, she didn't want to touch any surface with her bare hands.

Potter led her to an open door halfway down the hall. "This was Ashley's."

The room was spartan. The single bed had been stripped of sheets exposing a dingy, stained mattress. Walking into the room, Pam surveyed the dresser and nightstand, both covered with a layer of dust. She quickly confirmed that the dresser was empty except for one odd sock. The nightstand's one drawer appeared empty. Pam removed it entirely and found a baggie of marijuana taped to the back.

"That ain't mine," Potter blurted as soon as he recognized the packet of weed. "My drug of choice is alcohol."

Pocketing the marijuana, Pam returned to the dresser and removed each drawer to check under and behind them. Not finding anything, she moved to the closet, with its door ajar. It was empty except for a jigsaw puzzle box showing a picture of cats playing cards. On the top shelf was a Monopoly game. She opened each of the boxes and found only what the covers indicated.

With her hands on her hips, Pam stared at the rest of the room. She got on her hands and knees to look under the bed. Dust bunnies were all that was visible in the beam of her flashlight.

Potter looked around the space and shook his head. "There's nothing else of hers in here."

"Can I see the bathroom she used?"

Potter didn't move from the door. "There's only one bathroom, and I cleaned out all of her stuff years ago."

"Maybe there's a hairbrush or some tweezed eyebrow hairs in a drawer."

"Ain't nothing like that there, only a sink and bathtub. You can go now."

Suspecting that the bathroom might be even more disgusting than the rest of the house, Pam didn't press the issue. She walked to the front door and paused with her hand on the knob. "We'll let you know when the M.E. confirms her identity."

Potter shrugged. "You can save your breath. I don't give a shit."

"Will you be making the funeral arrangements?"

Potter snorted. "Cremate her and send the box to her husband."

Not wanting to reveal that Satter was in jail, Pam nodded. "Thanks for your time."

"Don't bother coming back. I probably won't answer the door."

* * *

After weighing the value of returning to the grisly recovery scene, or moving on with identifying Ashley's remains, Pam decided she needed to speak with Satter in order to get their dentist's name. She called the courthouse and spoke with the jail. "Put Casey Satter in an interview room. I'll be there in twenty minutes, let him stew until I get there."

The jailer chuckled. "No problem."

Pam found Theo Jacoby, a burly jailer, standing in the hallway outside the row of interview rooms. He nodded to her. "Do you want me inside or out?"

"Stand in the corner and look ominous."

Theo smiled and opened the door. "I can do that."

Satter looked up when the door opened. Seeing Pam, he scowled. "What do *you* want?"

Pam took the chair across from him, steeling herself for the interview. "Mr. Satter, can I ask you a question? Did you not file a missing person's report for Ashley because you knew she was at the bottom of a well or because you put her there?" She waited for him to dig himself a hole.

Satter glared at Pam and didn't disappoint her. "How the hell was I supposed to know where she was? She was out screwing around on me! She cleaned out our joint account and hightailed it out of town. There was no reason for me to report her missing. I couldn't file a theft report on a joint bank account!" he spat at her. All at once, her words sank in, and his once smug face became uncertain. "A well? Ashley was in a well?"

Pam knew at that moment Casey had nothing to do with Carter Miller dumping Ashley into the Amish well. She changed tracks and ignored his question. She leaned her elbows on the table. "Casey, I'm the person who's been watching your drone videos. I know who you've been blackmailing. Your victims are lining up to testify against you." Pam nodded toward the door. "As soon as I'm through with you, I have to talk to the three of them waiting in the other interview rooms."

Casey's smile became smug once again. "No one is going to testify against me. They won't come forward to testify against their blackmailer."

"It's interesting that you think that. Blackmail is extortion, a much higher-level crime than, say, dumping appliances in the ditch, or running an unlicensed kennel. The county attorney is entertaining offers of immunity to people who've committed petty crimes in return for their testimony in your multiple-count felony extortion case," she fibbed.

Hearing about two of his victims caused the color to drain from Casey's face.

"Do I have your attention?"

"I want my lawyer."

Pam stood and nodded. "No problem. Do you want me to show him the drone footage of your extortion operation before or after you talk to him? Oh, and the Peeping Tom video you took of a sheriff's deputy?" Theo opened the door and Pam stopped halfway through. "By the way, who's your dentist?"

"My dentist?"

"Yes, your dentist."

Satter frowned and shook his head. "What does Dr. Palmer have to do with my case?"

"He's got nothing at all to do with your case. However, he might be able to help us identify Ashley's remains."

Outside of the interview room, Theo smiled. "You played him perfectly."

Pam smiled. "Thanks, Theo. You can take him back to his cell."

Pam took a step away but was stopped by the jailer. "Pam?"

She turned and asked, "Yeah?"

"Did you notice how Satter went white when you mentioned the kennel and appliance dumping? You scared the shit out of him. Bakken might get him to take a plea deal."

"I hope not, Theo. I'd hate to have the residents of Pine County miss out on the grisly details revealed during their favorite realtor's extortion trial."

Epilogue

Pam, Travis, and Noah were the last of the moving crew to arrive at CJ's apartment. Pam brought Noah inside while Travis backed the pickup into a spot near the entrance. She held the door as Eddie and Sandy carried a dresser down the steps. Behind them, Mary and Floyd carried boxes carefully labeled with their contents.

"It's about time you showed up," Sandy kidded Pam as they passed. "Luckily, there's still some heavy things to load."

Grinning, Pam replied, "My job is keeping Noah from getting underfoot."

"Someone grab the dog!" CJ yelled from inside as Bailey rushed out the apartment door, turned, then waddled down the steps. While holding Noah's hand, Pam lunged toward the dog, grabbing her collar as she passed. Bailey's momentum jerked Pam off her feet and she tumbled backwards.

CJ bounded down the stairs and pounced on the basset, who was trying to pull Pam out of the apartment building entrance door. Noah laughed and bounced with excitement as the two women struggled to maintain control of the squirming dog.

The escape attempt ended when Travis arrived, scooping up Bailey in his arms. "Sorry girl, it's moving day, and we don't have time to chase you around town."

Brushing dust off of her jeans and composing herself, Pam asked, "It looks like Floyd and Sandy's pickups are already loaded. What else is left?"

"The couch, TV cabinet, and the coffee table are about the end of the furniture. And there are still lots of boxes we can use to fill in any open spaces. If we don't have room for all the boxes, I can get the last ones when I come back to clean," CJ stated.

Pam and Noah followed CJ up the short stairway as she led Bailey back to the second floor apartment. "Are you excited?"

Shaking her head, CJ stood in the nearly empty living room. "I'm mostly exhausted. It'll be nice to get the bed set up so I can get a decent night's sleep."

"You've had insomnia?" Pam asked as Travis carried the coffee table past them.

"It's not insomnia. Bailey senses that there's something going on. She's been on the bed, off the bed, snoring, farting, howling, and generally making a nuisance of herself for a week. It'll be nice to get her into the new house where she can get out in her own yard without someone having to walk her. That'll give me time to unpack and arrange the furniture."

Sandy walked into the apartment and paused next to Eddie. "I think the couch has to go into Travis' truck next, then the TV cabinet. We can pack other boxes on top of them."

Pam picked up the toddler. "I'd like to help but I think Noah and I will just supervise."

Floyd and Mary joined Pam and Noah, who were watching the last boxes being carried from the apartment. Mary picked up Noah as Floyd leaned close to Pam and whispered, "The County Attorney's Office began grand jury proceedings in Raster's case."

"That's what I expected."

Floyd chuckled.

"I suppose anyone who'd run over his wife with a Bobcat, get out to make sure she was dead, then run over her again, is a real nut case." Pam froze when she realized what she'd just said. "He's not going for an insanity defense, is he?"

"The video establishes his mental state. He was fully aware of his actions and their consequences. Besides, I'm sure the court will order a Rule 20 evaluation in order to rule that out. As you know, Satter has been charged with several additional felonies, including possession of a controlled substance. He won't be selling houses any time soon."

Mary leaned close and said, "Travis just carried out the last box and CJ is ready to lock up. You two need to stop the shop talk and take this young man to Bailey's new house."

* * *

With full plates of picnic food, everyone settled down in lawn chairs around the fire pit at the house. CJ was overwhelmed with gratitude when she thought of all they had done to help her move into her new home. She glanced around, making sure the basset wasn't chasing a rabbit or digging another hole before she cleared her throat to make her announcement.

"Everyone, I'm so thankful," she glanced in Bailey's direction, "Correction. WE are so thankful for all that you've done for us. Especially when I decided to buy a house from a felon," she rolled her eyes upward and whispered, "I know, Bobby," then met snorts from her friends with her own. She raised her glass of lemonade and continued, "None of this would have been possible without every one of you. Bailey and I would like to announce the arrival of our new roommate next week."

CJ looked from face to face. Most held looks of confusion mixed with wonder. Pam nudged Eddie with the tip of her tennis shoe and winked at him. Floyd was speechless and Eddie shook his head vehemently in response to the five sets of eyes that eventually turned and rested expectantly in his direction.

"No! Not Eddie," CJ chortled. She slapped her hand on her jeans and pointed in the direction of the overgrown pasture surrounding the pole shed. "Clover will live over there. He's got dreamy brown eyes and silky auburn hair," CJ sighed.

"You're buying a HORSE? Did you knock your head when you took Satter down in the hallway the other day? Why the hell didn't you tell me? And what the hell is wrong with you?" Pam bellowed.

"Calm down, girl. Just think of all the free pony rides for Noah."

Floyd began to laugh. And laugh. And snort. Then, he looked at Eddie's stunned face and howled even harder.

Mary tapped his shoulder and whispered, "That's enough, honey. The poor guy is already embarrassed."

Pam and Travis whispered, then cleaned up Noah, who'd smeared his face with mayo while eating potato salad with his fingers. Pam walked to CJ. "This is a nice place. You'll be happy here."

CJ hugged Pam, Travis, and Noah and then turned to the others. "So, my next question is," her eyes sparkled. "Who wants to help stack hay for next winter?"

The End

***Other Dean L. Hovey mysteries from
BWL Publishing Inc.***

Whistling Pines cozies

Whistling up a Ghost
Whistling Pirates
Whistling Bake Off
Whistling Artist
Whistling Fireman
Whistling Wedding
Whistling Librarian (Late 2025)

Doug Fletcher mysteries

Stolen Past
Washed Away
Dead in the Water
Death in Shifting Sands
Devils Fall
Prairie Menace
Down River

Burnt Evidence
Gator Bait
Grave Survey
Dead End Trail
The Last Rodeo
Peril in Paradise
Western Justice
Medora Murder
A Bourbon to Die For (2025)

Pine County Mysteries

Killer Secrets
Deadly Mixture
Fatal Business
Taxed to Death
Conflict of Interest
Skidded and Skunked

Dean Hovey is the award-winning and best-selling author of three mystery series. He uses his scientific background, travel, extensive research, and consultants to add reality and depth to his stories. One reader said Dean's characters are like people he'd like to invite over for a beer and discussion. Hovey's Doug Fletcher mysteries follow U.S. National Park Service investigators Doug and Jill Fletcher as their investigations take them to national parks from coast to coast. The Whistling Pines mysteries are humorous cozies set in a northern Minnesota senior residence, following Peter Rogers, the Whistling Pines recreation director, as he stumbles through the investigation of murders in his small town. The Pine County mystery series follows sheriff's deputies Pam Ryan, Floyd Swenson, and CJ Jensen as they investigate murders in rural Minnesota. Dean and his wife split their year between northern Minnesota and Arizona.

D.L. Dixen makes her home on a small hobby farm with her family, ponies and basset hound, not far from the Pine County border. Her professional background ranges from the criminal justice system to secondary English education. Her professional experiences and deep familial Pine County roots make for good fiction in the Pine County mystery series. Skidded and Skunked is her first mystery.

www.ingramcontent.com/pod-product-compliance
Lightning Source LLC
Chambersburg PA
CBHW072354110726

47909CB00003B/695